AFFLICTION

ASSA
RAYMOND
BAKER

GOOD 2 GO PUBLISHING

AFFLICTION
Written by Assa Raymond Baker
Cover Design: Davida Baldwin Odd Ball Designs
Typesetter: Mychea
ISBN: 978-1-947340-44-2
Copyright © 2019 Good2Go Publishing
Published 2019 by Good2Go Publishing
7311 W. Glass Lane • Laveen, AZ 85339
www.good2gopublishing.com
https://twitter.com/good2gobooks
G2G@good2gopublishing.com
www.facebook.com/good2gopublishing
www.instagram.com/good2gopublishing

AFFLICTION

In the mean streets of Milwaukee, a.k.a. Killwaukee, everybody has a legal or illegal hustle. It's no different for Fame, a thorough hit-man, and his beautiful drug-dealing love interest at the moment, Promiss. The secret lives of these two young lovers threatens the one they hope to build together, as well as Danny Boy's, a young jack boy whose a member of a violent gang of goons with a love for taking that almighty dollar from wherever and whoever has it. But when an assassination attempt fails, the hot gossipy streets cause Fame to burn the city down and set Danny Boy off on a rampage to find out the truth. Then when Promiss's ex-lover suddenly shows up on her doorstep one morning, Fame's world is turned upside down.

PROLOGUE

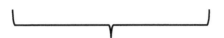

Two disciplined thugs sat inside a deep-green
Buick LeSabre watching the entrance of a small
buzzing night club. They were there for the owner of
a multi-colored, shiny blue army-fatigue-painted
motorcycle that was currently parked at the far end
of the block. It was now a little before one in the
morning, and Fame hoped the target would call it a
night soon so they could get the hit over with. He
wanted to get back to Milwaukee and hopefully into
the arms of the beauty who was talking softly in his
ear.

"It's about time your ass off the phone!" Slim
complained, aligning himself in the driver's seat to

face his friend. "Don't let me have to revoke your G-card. You know you're not supposed to sit on the phone like that with something new."

"What? Bro, if she falling asleep on the phone with me and shit, I know she's feeling me the way I'm trying to fuck with her. So what's the damn difference if I wait to talk to her or limit our time on the phone?" asked Fame after ending his call and putting the phone in the zip-up pocket of his black Burberry hoodie.

"Bruh, the difference is what's there and what's not. How long you been fuckin' with ole girl, and you still ain't got no pussy? Fam, you trippin'."

"Naw, I ain't trippin'. If you didn't need me up here to help you catch this lil white boy, I'd be somewhere fuckin her brains out right now."

"This about that cash, though. MOB 'til the world blow up! My nigga, you know when a nigga got the paper there's bad bitches around you like air, but when you down all you got is your hand and hot oil . . ."

"Hold that thought," Fame interrupted. "There he go. Meet me at the corner so we can get the fuck outta here without none of them other drunk muthafuckas seeing the car."

With that, Fame eased out of the right rear door, staying low so as not to bring attention to them from the small crowd that quickly formed outside of the club. The focused thug briskly went after the skinny, illegal fentanyl dealer, who had to have pissed his plug off to have the nice bounty put on his head.

Fame followed as far as he could from the opposite side of the block, but when his target got a few feet from the bike he dashed across the street. He wanted to be as close as he could be before upping the gun and pulling the trigger. Fame wasn't worried all that much about being noticed, or standing out to anyone, because him and the target were both dressed in black hooded pullovers and jeans. The only difference besides their skin color was that they were carrying. The skinny, slightly staggering target held a black helmet with writing on it that matched his motorcycle. Fame held a silenced Glock 23, concealed by the shadow of the way he held it close to his thigh as he moved.

"Aye, excuse me, fam?" As soon as the unsuspecting man spun to respond, Fame pulled the trigger, hitting him with two quick and muffled slugs in the face. Then he ran off as fast as he could back to the car.

CHAPTER 1

Promiss pulled herself from the best night's rest she'd had all month. She would've stayed in the super-plush king-sized bed all day had it not been for a full bladder. The hotel room was the most luxurious one she had ever slept alone in throughout her life. A bit reluctant, Promiss rolled from beneath the warm comforter, stretching loudly as she lazily marched into the bathroom. After relieving herself, Promiss filled the whirlpool, opting to take a soothing morning bath instead of standing under the large round shower head and having the hot pulsating water come down on her the way she had the day before, right after she'd checked in.

The well-deserved mini-vacation was all because Promiss released the pain of her last boyfriend to make room for a new man in her busy life. Almost an hour later, Promiss emerged from the bathroom refreshed, with a strong desire to be held by Fame. She thought of his unpredictable schedule as she opened the room's curtains with the remote to let the natural light flow in through the infinity window. The view of the city was much different from above. She turned on the radio and increased the volume, feeling the song "Anything" by SZA:

Maybe I should kill my inhibition, Maybe I'll be perfect in a new dimension, Maybe I should pray a little harder, Or work a little smarter

Promiss sang along while moisturizing her Janell

Monae-like—only slightly darker complected—sexy physique. Her friends and family said that Promiss looked like the singer/actress, but she didn't see it in her reflection in the mirror.

This time, baby, I promise I have learned my lesson, ooh,

Down for the ride, down for the ride,

You could take me anywhere

Promiss giggled while she sang, thinking about how she agreed without a moment's hesitation when Fame asked her to spend a few days with him in the luxurious suite.

Keepin' up is hard to do,

Even harder feeling heavy, steady chasin' you,

Baby, why are you lookin' around, you lonely?

I feel you comin' down like honey,

Do do you even know I'm alive?

Do do you even know I, I

The beeping and buzzing of her cellphone on the bed alerted her to a text from Fame. She quickly scooped it up and read the text.

"Good morning, beautiful. I hope you slept good since you fell asleep on the phone—LOL. Dress casually. I'll be downstairs waiting on you for breakfast."

"OMG, I'm sooo sorry. LOL. Why don't you come up?"

"Just got back and I'm hungry. If I come up, I won't eat, unless you plan to be my breakfast?" Then, "I'm downstairs now. Wud up?"

"Too fast. LOL. I'm not ready. See you at breakfast," Promiss replied, then retrieved her Prada overnight bag and put one of the three outfits she brought along for the stay. She checked herself over in the full-body-length mirror once she was ready. Dressed in a form-fitting, Citizens of Humanity denim jumpsuit, casual brown leather Van's sneakers, and the original print universal Louis Vuitton bag that she knew would complement anything she wore, Promiss headed down to the hotel lobby.

As soon as she stepped off the uninterrupted descent of the smooth elevator ride, Fame was right there waiting. His handsome face and Michael B. Jordan build made the casual outfit he was wearing look expensive. Promiss immediately noticed other women checking him out and wondered whether Fame dressed himself in the soft cotton short-sleeved polo, white with multi-color blue and forest-green stripes, dark blue khaki pants, and loose-strung mid-top Levi canvas shoes, or if he had a girlfriend he wasn't telling her about. She made plans to get all of her questions answered over their meal.

"Good morning, you!" she greeted when he crossed the lobby to meet her.

"Seeing you right now just made it better," Fame flirted, stopping right in front of her. "I ain't gon' lie, I thought you was gonna be another thirty or forty-five minutes."

"Ha ha, I know you did." She hugged him and

got a whiff of the Versace Men's fragrance. Being in his arms made her wonder if he had a girl at home or not. Was she going to lay him and send him home, or put it on his fine ass so he'd never leave? "I fooled yo' ass, didn't I?" She laughed, allowing Fame to take her hand and lead the way into the dining room.

When they were seated, they talked over a light breakfast that neither finished because they were too caught up learning about all the things they had in common. Afterward they went for a walk, using the time for window shopping and talking to get closer. Promiss admired Fame's knowledge of Old Milwaukee. They continued to leisurely stroll east toward the lakefront, with him doing most of the talking because of her questions.

"Promiss, it's okay to tell me to shut the fuck up." He smiled.

"No, I don't mind. I think it's cute. With all you know about these buildings and places, you should be in construction."

"Or a tour guide," he joked, then went on commenting on the variety of changes all of Milwaukee had made during the thirty months he did in the Dodge Correctional Institution for felony receiving stolen property. Fame explained that he had bought a GMC Sierra pickup from a white woman who was strung out on drugs and sold the truck without her husband's permission.

"That's fucked up," was all Promiss could say when he finished the story. All she could see about

Fame told her that he was everything women who liked bad boys dreamed of. He was good looking, independent, intelligent, and knew his way around a toolbox. She'd found out how handy Fame was the first night they'd met. Her old Chrysler had broken down, and he just so happened to be doing some work on a truck in a garage nearby . . .

"Hellooo, excuse me, sir!" Promiss called out, expecting to see a much older face to appear from underneath the vehicle.

"Yeah, whassup?" Fame responded, simultaneously sliding away from the project.

"Oooh, well my car won't start. I already know it's the battery; I just don't know where to put the new one."

"Where's your car? I can check it out for you real fast," he told her, checking her out from head to toe and liking every inch of what stood in front of him.

"It's right here in the middle of the alley," she answered, giving him a shy smile. " I tried to let it coast as far as I could when I seen your light on down here."

"Where you coming from that you seen me?" he asked, walking over to push the car the twenty to thirty feet it was away from where he was working. Fame kicked himself inside for not being aware of the car stopping so close to him in the dark alley.

"Buying a new battery. It's on the floor in the back, and before you ask, I did ask the guy at the parts store if he could put it in after he told me I needed a new one."

"So what happened that he didn't do it for you?" he asked, popping the hood of the car. "He said he didn't know where it was at, so he gave me a boost so I could get home, but it stopped just as I was turning into the driveway," she answered, pointing down the alley.

"Whoever the nigga was at the store lied to you or needs to find another job. Look, the battery right here." He waved her over to where he was and pointed out the battery's location. "He just didn't wanna do it cuz you gotta take all of this stuff off to get down to it," Fame explained, waving the flashlight.

"Ooooh, damn, can you do it?"

"Yeah, I got you. It's not like I was busy or nothing." He smiled. "You can stand in there out of the rain if you want."

Promiss took him up on the offer, not wanting the light mist to mess up her hair or her phone. She watched him make quick work of swapping out the batteries, impressed because Fame didn't look like the grease-monkey type.

"All done," he announced, closing the hood. "You needed oil, so I put it in for you too."

"Alright, how much do I owe you?" she asked, starting the car to check his work.

"Let me seeee." He pretended to add numbers in the air with his dirty fingers for a second. "Just give me like $500," he joked, then laughed at the shocked

expression on her face. "I'm just playin', but you can

give me your number, or just take mine and promise

to call me."

CHAPTER 2

Now two months later she was out walking hand in hand with him along the boat docks. She liked everything about him. Fame was perfect for her, just too good to be true, so she asked him again why he didn't have a girlfriend.

"I . . . Okay, here's the uncut truth. I do got a girl, and I'm not letting you go for nobody." He pulled her closer.

"Stop playing and tell me why ain't nobody got you cuffed up."

"Okay, since you won't drop it, I was engaged before I went to prison, and after a few months, we grew apart. But really, she couldn't take it and just abandoned me. She tried to get back with me when I needed her most, but it's fuck her now. And I ain't got with nobody else like that because my life's just too complicated for most females. If it wasn't because of your understanding of the hours I keep at work, we wouldn't be here right now. So that's it. You happy?"

Promiss could see Fame's honesty in his eyes and fell for him a little more. She volunteered the information about her past relationships. She admitted that she could never really find a man who didn't get on nonsense with her because she sometimes worked long hours and liked to have free time with her friends and family. Promiss found it easy to open up to him.

"So who do you really be with when you go outta town? I know it's someone you fuckin' on?" she probed for the last time.

"I'm not really into white girls, and that's pretty much all that's around when I'm working besides my clients, and I never mix business like that. I take my job very seriously. If I don't it's easy for people to get hurt," he answered, then changed the subject.

Promiss just smiled at him, flirtatiously running her hand down his arm as she leaned into him. She wanted to kiss him but didn't know how he would react to it. In her experience with the men she dated, none of them liked displaying their affection to her in public—not even holding hands like they were doing now. It felt nice, so she didn't press her luck.

Fame saw something in her eyes and felt the warm vibe between them. He stopped in the middle of the block and leaned down and pressed his lips to hers. His excitement rose to a new height when she kissed him back. It was delicious. Promiss almost let herself melt in his strong arms. Neither of them wanted the kiss to end, and both of them wished they were someplace more private.

They were just standing there staring into each other's eyes like the new lovers they were, when suddenly a stampede of hot lead set off pandemonium all around them. Promiss watched in horror as the innocent Burt Reynolds-looking fisherman a few feet away had his head slammed to his shoulder violently, splattering blood and memories everywhere. Without a second hesitation, Fame pulled Promiss to the ground while quickly scanning the area where he heard the gunfire coming from. He caught sight of the young shooter just as he was taking aim and firing in their direction again.

Bullets flew inches over Fame's head, breaking the ground all around him and Promiss. Years' worth of being in the streets was what had prevented Fame from leaving his gun in the car when he pulled up at the hotel earlier. If his father didn't do anything else, he taught Fame to be ready for whatever. Rolling away from Promiss after pushing her safely behind a wide, short concrete post, he drew his trusty .380 and returned fire in the inexperienced shooter's direction.

The shots missed the target, only hitting parked cars, but were close enough to send the would-be assassin running.

Past provoked, Fame jumped to his feet and sprinted after him. He pushed people out of his path as he ran. Promiss screamed for Fame not to chase him, but he was too far away, and mad, to hear her. She caught her breath, then tried to get up, wincing in pain from the twisted ankle she'd gotten when Fame pushed her. She still got up and stood on it for a moment. It was good enough for her to walk on it. Promiss dragged after Fame the best she could.

There were too many innocent people between Fame and his target for him to keep shooting at him. He didn't want to hit a civilian, so he dropped the gun in his pocket to make sure he wouldn't drop it during the chase or be the first to be shot when the police showed up. Just as he did, the man he was after collided hard into a steel bike rack. The punk's gun was knocked out of his hand when he crashed to the ground. As soon as he got halfway up on his feet, Fame tackled him, sending them both crashing into a park bench before rolling to the ground.

The dazed thug quickly scooped up a handful of sand and tossed it into Fame's face, followed by a hard fist as they wrestled murderously in front of the nosey, startled spectators. Promiss caught up to the scene in time to see the shooter shove Fame off him and get to his feet. Instead of taking off running again, the shooter threw a wild haymaker at Fame's head. He dodged it, countering with a savage combination of fists and knees. As Fame battered the man's face and body, he slipped on a rock, giving the shooter time to hit Fame with a roundhouse kick that knocked him off his feet. The shooter was off and running before Fame hit the ground.

Promiss rushed over to him just as he drew his gun again.

"Fame!" she shouted, making him stop from pulling the trigger. "It's too many people out here." She helped him to his feet.

"Is you alright? You're bleeding." He panicked, pulling her top open to get a better look at where the blood was coming from on her side.

Promiss was too concerned about Fame's well-being the whole time to even know she was hurt anyplace else besides her ankle.

"Arghhh!"

"Promiss, it don't look like it went in. It might be just a bad flesh wound. Didn't you feel it?"

"No, not until now," she answered through her teeth with tears now running down her cheeks.

Fame patted himself down for his phone but found that he had lost it somewhere. Promiss still had her purse strapped over her shoulder, so he told her to call an ambulance for herself, and at the sound of approaching first response vehicles he gave her his word that he would catch up with her at the hotel.

CHAPTER 3

It was a struggle to leave her like he did, but he was still on parole, and the shooting alone would've gotten him thrown back in prison just for being there. Fame fled, trying not to attract more unwanted attention to himself. He removed the bloody, dirty shirt and slowed to a power walk. He made it the more than half-dozen blocks back to the hotel with approaching police sirens in the distance and an ambulance racing down the street, back in the direction of where he'd left Promiss standing.

Making it safely back to the hotel, Fame retrieved his keycard and work phone from his car, then went straight to the room and showered. He used the time to think and get his thoughts together, wondering if he was making the right move being in this room right now when the police were surely out looking for all parties involved in the chaos. One thing he knew for sure: Promiss was somewhere being thoroughly questioned. He thought of how she'd watched him leave her, hurt, crying, and alone.

Fame was standing in front of the mirror, nursing minor wounds that he'd received at the hands of the unknown thug, when he heard Promiss enter the room. Knowing she was near made his heart flutter, kicking up steamy thoughts of asking her to get back in the shower with him. The truth was Fame didn't know how Promiss felt about him now after almost being killed and left to deal with things on her own. But she came back. So maybe he still had a chance with her, or maybe she just had returned to collect her belongings and some answers about what had happened at the lakefront.

"How can I explain anything when I don't fuckin' know who was shooting at me?" he asked his reflection in the foggy mirror. "I can promise Promiss one thing, that on my life I'ma find out and handle it." He wrapped himself in a towel before walking out of the bathroom to see her. When her eyes met his, Fame expected to find anger in them, but instead all he saw was nervous shyness. "Heey, I didn't hear you come in," he lied.

"I just got here. I tried to get here sooner, but the

police were all over me about the shooting because a witness told 'em they seen me with you."

"Hmm, damn."

"Fame, don't trip. I didn't tell them bitches shit about you. I just told them basically I was in the wrong place at the wrong time, and I didn't know the person who saved my life. I gave 'em a bogus description, and they told me to call if I remember anything more. They offered me a ride here, but I declined and took a cab just in case they wanted to check the room or check the log-ins," Promiss explained. She hoped but was doubtful that Fame would still want to fool with her after she almost got him killed.

Promiss guessed the hit was meant for her

because of the part of her life she hadn't shared with him.

"That's good thinkin', but my name ain't on the room. My nigga's wifey plugged us with it. She always tryin' to play matchmaker an' shit. But we do need to talk."

"Fame, I know, but I'm not in the mood right now. Can we do it after I take a shower and wash this day off me? I just need some time to sit back and chill," Promiss told him, hoping his sexy ass wouldn't press the issue until she knew what to say.

"I understand. Let's just chill for now."

Promiss released the breath she was holding, then put on her best smile before walking into the bathroom. The air was still warm from Fame's shower, and it made her think of their kiss. "I should go back in there and snatch that towel off and give him something to make him forget his name," she whispered in the mirror as she undressed and stepped under the soothing water as the volcano between her thighs awakened. After about ten minutes or so Fame asked her how bad the wound on her side was. "It's not bad, but I need you to help me rewrap my ankle when I get out." She wanted to give him something better to look forward to but didn't want to mess up with him any more than she already had.

"I don't think you was supposes to take that off so soon, Promiss, so get up outta there so I can put it back before you can't walk on it at all."

The stern voice Fame used with her was a turn-on. She didn't hesitate fulfilling his order. "Okay, I'm getting out now. My ankle's alright. I don't feel it because of the pain meds they gave me, so don't worry." She smiled, wrapping her dripping body in a towel before walking into the bedroom. "Dang, that felt good. I could've stayed in there for an hour."

Promiss found Fame still with just a towel on, sitting on the bed, staring out the window overlooking the city. His hearty well-developed, half-naked body was better than she'd pictured it would be.

"I didn't feel like putting on my dirty clothes," he explained when he saw the way she was looking at him.

"I ain't say nothing. I understand, and we're

grown. Seeing each other like this was gonna happen sooner or later, right?" She stopped and stood smiling inches in front of him.

"Yeah, I can't say I ain't thought about it and then some," he admitted, almost sliding himself up her body as he stood up. If Promiss was going to leave, she would've already.

Fame knew she wanted answers, but that wasn't the need he saw in her pretty brown eyes. Without a second guess he pressed his lips to hers. When she didn't pull away, he enveloped her in his powerful arms and kissed her deeper. Promiss felt his length harden as he held her, and pressed herself into it, wanting to feel it all inside her. When his hands cupped her ass, she let out a soft moan of encouragement and dragged her nails down his chest. Lost in the feeling of her soft lips, Fame pushed his tongue between them and danced his tongue around with hers.

The kiss was heaven in a bottle to them both. His harness throbbed to be buried and covered with her wetness. Fame slid his hands under her towel to feel her soft warm skin. Then he scooped her off her feet. Promiss wrapped her legs around him, and her towel fell away as soon as he laid her on the bed. Fame stood up, taking a moment to admire her before dropping his towel. He kissed up her right leg and slowly pushed her legs farther and farther apart. Promiss clawed the bed, loving the sensual sensation of the skilled mouth traveling up her body. His warm breath on her moist mound caused her back to arch.

"Ooooh God, babe, yesss!"

Fame smiled but moved on, teasingly not doing what she expected of him. His mouth soon found her nipples. He sucked and tickled them with his tongue, while at the same time rubbing his hardness against her morning-shaved pussy. He propped himself over her on his fists so he could watch her expression as he slid inside of her warmth. She was so hot and tight he was unable to slow himself as he forcefully pounded in and out of her. Promiss furiously clawed his shoulders and back, loving the pain-laced pleasure as he gave her the nice hard fuck she needed. She pulled him down on top of her, holding him tightly as she came in waves, clenching his length until she felt him bust buried deep inside her.

He collapsed beside her, out of breath and sweaty.

Neither one of them said a word about the shooting,

not wanting to mess up how they were feeling in that

moment. Soon they were both asleep in each other's

arms.

CHAPTER 4

Awakened by the radiating pain from her injuries, and the guilt that went with them, Promiss tried to quietly ease out of the bed, right away hating her decision to peel away from the warm body beside her. She scooped up her abandoned phone and overnight bag and went into the bathroom to get dressed and check her messages. Promiss swallowed a couple of the powerful pain pills before dressing in fitted jeans and a T-shirt. She cursed to herself about the info her cousin texted her that could've led to the attempt on her life, and the reason Promiss was sneaking away from her new man, not to mention the

much-deserved personal time. "Bring me something back to eat," I'm hungry,"

Fame whispered in a low drowsy voice that made

Promiss freeze at the door.

"Alright, go back to sleep," she answered before

slipping out the exit and heading home.

Promiss drove past the location of the shootout

and in the direction the man ran. As she followed the

route, she thought of all the gunfire that took place

before Fame shot back. "It was two of them bitches!"

she yelled aloud inside her car, then sped toward her

sister's place.

~ ~ ~

"Endure? Bitch, what the fuck did you do?"

Promiss snapped at her sister as she slammed the door hard enough for a family photo to fall crashing to the floor.

"Bitch, don't be coming up in here tearing up my shit!" she shouted, irritated by the morning drama.

"Bitch, don't play dumb. That 'H' shit you got out here almost got me killed yesterday," Promiss explained, limping over to the navy-blue-and-gold sofa chaise and sitting down to take pressure off her foot.

"Oh my God, Promiss, I didn't know. Mama just told me you got shot down by the lake and the police was questioning you. I texted and called you, but you didn't answer. She thought it had something to do with that mystery man you was with. Who told you about what I'm doing anyway?" Endure inquired, kneeling and picking up the framed photo out of the shards of glass.

"Don't worry who told me, just know I know."

"Well know that I won't make moves that won't pay off. I'm trying to make us a few hundred thousand right quick, so work with me, bitch?"

"Sis, you should've talked to us before you made moves. You're taking a big risk with a lot of our money. And look what happened already. I was shot, Endure, shot!"

Right then Endure's cellphone started playing their cousin's set ringtone. She picked it up off the stand and answered it with a calm, "What up?"

"This Shay," she exclaimed, giggling like she

was wasted.

"I know who you is. What you in this fuckin' early?" asked Endure ready to scold her.

Shay managed two of the family's elderly living homes. She was also responsible for keeping 105 pounds of weed moving through the West Lawn Projects on a regular basis.

"Yeah, bitch, I'm chopped, but listen, I got word from a reliable bitch that fools with Roc off the east. He said he selling his loud way cheaper than ours, and it's that bag too."

"Oookay, how reliable is ole girl?" Endure asked, checking the time on her icy Omega watch.

"It's a he not a she, and he very reliable. He got a baby by Roc's sister.

How do you want me to handle this?"

"I don't want you to do nothing right now but find out if Roc had anything to do with what happened to Promiss. We gonna handle the rest."

"I got you. Tell Promiss to get up with me. I'm trying to hear about her new boo," Shay said before ending the call.

"Shay's ass always fuckin' with somebody's man," Promiss said, shaking her head and fishing her pain meds out of her bag.

"Yeah, that's how she stays constantly ahead of muthafuckas."

"Why didn't you tell her to send them boys down there to handle Roc? We was good to his fool ass and he went behind our back pulling this shit?" Promiss exclaimed, grinding her teeth the way she always did when she was upset.

"Because I didn't. I got something else in mind." Endure shrugged.

"Fuck your plans, Endure. Send them down there!" Promiss ordered, slamming her pill bottle down on the coffee table. "Don't test me, bitch, or I'll knock your ass out!"

"Whatever, broke-leg bitch. I wanna see this trick. Come on, hop over here and bust a move," Endure dared her, walking over and standing right in front of where Promiss was still sitting.

Promiss knew she was in no condition to fight with her slightly taller little sister. She also knew that once Endure was provoked, it was hard to calm her down. She was the type that didn't stop fighting until the other was down and bloody, but they were sisters and things never went that far between them.

"How much money do we got out there?" Promiss inquired, choosing to ignore the dare. "Or do you even know?"

Endure just stared at Promiss with her perfect lace wig. Not one strand of her hair was ever seen out of place, not even when she was reaching around Milwaukee in her shiny black Lexus coup with the top down. Endure was a little envious of her sister. Their mother made Promiss the CEO of the family business, and since then New Living Center had grown to what it now was under Promiss's watchful eye. Their mother got things started from selling weed, which the sisters continued to do.

"Yeah, I know, but tell you for what? Promiss, you know you already know everything. And you know you already know everything. And you know I gave it to Sharky to get off down on the eastside," she said, rolling her eyes.

"I didn't know Sharky was on the east. Do he fool with Roc?"

"No, but we got two spots in this hood that's doing numbers right now. That's why I don't wanna send our guys down there. All they gonna do is make it hot for Sharky down there," Endure explained.

"Okay, but you better be right about this shit. If Mama asks, it's all on you, just so you know."

"Yeah, I know." She smiled. "Sooo what

happened when you told your new boo that you almost got him killed?"

"I didn't tell him yet, and I snuck out on him this morning," Promiss answered, then fished her phone out of her bag to see if Fame tried to get in touch with her yet. Nope, no missed calls or texts.

"I knew you wouldn't. Now tell me, did you put it on him with your broke-leg ass the way I taught you?"

They talked until it was time for them to make their daily tours around the centers.

CHAPTER 5

A solid fist slammed into the cheek of an unconscious young man to arouse him. The hostage's vision was blurry and teary, but another punch helped him focus. Jon weakly shook off the sting of the blow and scanned his surroundings. It was all new to him. The last place he remembered being was standing on the block, talking to a pretty Jodie Comer-looking white girl from the hood.

~ ~ ~

"Wudup, ma, you tryna let me hit or what?" Jon asked between sips of Tonka gin that was being passed between the small group.

"Whatever, you can't handle this candy I got anyway. I heard about you, little man. I need something that's gonna fill me up," she clowned him, laughing with the others.

"Yeah right, ain't no bitch told you no shit like that about me. This here is 100 percent hung kong."

"Whatever. So you didn't take down Mandi two days ago behind her house in you—" Tonya screamed in mid-sentence when thugs with black-and-white bandanas covering half of their faces spilled out of a Dodge minivan.

The thugs pushed her out of the way and beat Jon unconscious as they pulled him inside the van.

~ ~ ~

Now Jon found himself in an unfamiliar

basement. He was bound to a chair by heavy tape, with a large sheet of clear plastic on the floor under his feet. He didn't know why he was there or what was going on, but from all of the movies he'd seen, if there was plastic covering the floor, that meant he wasn't going to make it out alive.

"Please don't hurt me, I didn't do nothing," Jon pleaded with the shadowy man behind the dim light. "Y'all got the wrong person. Please, I won't say nothing about this!"

"Naw, punk, it's you we want. Now shut the fuck up until we tell you to talk!" a bandana-covered face barked at him before hitting Jon on top of his already pounding head, sending a new wave of pain and dizziness through it.

Fame stood off to the right just out of the hostage's eyesight. He knew this wasn't the man he had fought with two days ago, but he could've been the driver or the second shooter that ran away first. One thing he knew for sure, Jon knew about the attempt on his life, and Fame planned on getting all of the information he could out of the man before he killed him.

About two hours ago Fame received a call from Byrd telling him that they had eyes on someone bragging about being the shooter. So Fame told him to have him snatched up so he could be questioned. Now Fame stepped in front of Jon, pulling on a pair of hard leather workman's gloves. He snapped right away, punching Jon repeatedly in the face. Blood splashed, running from various cuts on Jon's face, nose, and mouth.

"Who paid you to try to kill me? Tell me who paid you and who you were with that day, and I won't kill you," Fame promised.

"Fuck you!" Jon spat at him. "Fuck you, you bitch-ass nigg—" His words were cut off by Byrd's angry fist smashing into the side of his head. The blow was so hard it knocked Jon and the chair to the floor.

Two other goons in the room set him upright, but not before giving him several savage kicks to his body.

"Okay, okay, stop!" Jon screamed, pleading with his tormentors all surrounding him. "Okay, I'll tell you. Please don't kill me!" Jon saw that all of the faces were still covered with red and black, or black and white bandanas. This told him that if they were going to kill him it wouldn't matter if he saw them.

"I already told yo' dumb ass I ain't gonna kill you. But if you keep being disrespectful I'ma make your punk ass wish you were dead. Now tell me what I wanna know!" Fame demanded, allowing Jon to see his face after using the bandana to wipe off the spit.

"Danny Boy. Danny Boy did it, he told me some nigga of the north side paid him to do the hit, but somebody chased him when his gun jammed or some shit. I don't know, I wasn't there. It's just what he told me!"

"Who paid him?"

"I don't know who paid him the $2,500, but I know he didn't give him the rest of the money. On my life that's all I know."

"How can I find that nigga so he can tell me who paid him?" Byrd demanded, stepping from the shadows bare-faced.

"Man, please! Byrd, ya fuck with my big cousin. Please let me go. I won't tell her shit. Please, man!"

"I don't give a fuck what you tell that bitch nigga. How do we find Danny Boy, or do Karren know him?" asked Byrd, then punching Jon in the mouth to let him know he wasn't giving him a pass because he was fucking on his cousin.

All the blow did was make Jon understand that no matter what he said or didn't say to them, he wouldn't be alive to warn his friends, so he started mumbling a prayer to himself crying harder.

Fame knew they wouldn't be getting any more information out of him, so he gave the masked goons the okay to kill him. All Jon saw before he died was his killer's gold-toothed grin and the flash from his gun that was almost touching his nose.

"Aye, slim, when you done here can you pick Karren up from work for me? I ain't tryna be around her after this shit with her cousin."

"Yeah, I got you. Maybe I can get her talking about this nigga Danny Boy an' shit."

"Whatever do what you do. Just don't hurt her, bro."

"Don't trip, fam. I'ma play this shit smart so we

find out the full truth behind all this shit."

"Make sure you get at me later too."

CHAPTER 6

Endure arrived to work later than she usually came bouncing in. She had left her bounce at home somewhere this morning. Today she wasn't feeling well, her throat hurt, her head was pounding, and her stomach was upset. She called Promiss and asked her what she should do, and asked if she could get someone to come in for her since she clearly needed to be at home in bed.

"Girl, why did you take your ass in if you knew you were coming down with something?"

"I didn't feel this bad when I got up. I thought it would pass. I bet that breakfast sandwich I ate made it worse. But that wouldn't have my throat feeling like this, would it?"

"Nope, you got the flu it sounds like, and we don't need none of them old folks catching that shit. I just texted Tammi to come in for you. She said thanks, she needed the hours. So stay away from everybody until she gets there. I'll come check on you after my hair appointment," Promiss said.

Endure ended the call with her sister, then called her man to come give her a ride home. When she told Sharky about the incident at the lakefront where Promiss was shot and almost killed the other day, he wouldn't allow Endure to go out anywhere alone. After he dropped her off at work, Sharky had to go to a meeting with his connect, so he couldn't come take her home himself. He sent one of his loyal soldiers named Mister to do it and promised her he would come to the house as soon as he could, before rushing her off the phone.

Mister made it to Endure in less than an hour, but it took Tammi almost twice that before she made it there to relieve her. Endure and Mister rushed right out because they both knew Mister had to get back to doing his real work: managing the workers in the trap houses for his boss. Still he made sure she got home safely, and also did a full sweep of the house and its grounds, before leaving Endure alone. Not too many people knew Sharky's true home address, so for Mister to be called upon to handle this task was a big show of trust.

~ ~ ~

Thick clouds of kush smoke filled the air and lungs of four hard-hearted marauders, who were already upset because they missed a chance at robbing Jasso for the second time. Eshy, Danny Boy, Freebandz, and Boony had quickly moved on to a new target. They were now following Sharky's pearl-white Chevy Tahoe with a renewed sense of determination to feed their greed. When they first spotted the flashy SUV, they'd thought Sharky was the one driving it, but when it parked in a driveway beside a house on 104th and Kiehnan and emptied out, they knew it wasn't him, but one of the workers and a female. What the four of them didn't know was that they were being led to Sharky's home and safe house.

"Fam, what we doing?"

"We gonna stay on that nigga's heels for a minute," Eshy answered, then took a pull off the blunt. "He gotta take the truck back, so if you tryna get paid, you ain't gon' lose him like you did the last mark."

"Pass that; let me hit that shit there fam," Danny Boy said, and Eshy passed him the blunt. "Aye, y'all, that nigga bitch was thick as hell. I might have to bend back and get at her, fam, straight up."

"On my Mama G, that bitch was bad, but what you gonna do, sit outside her crib until she come out? Yeah, that's it, nigga, you stalk the bitch," Freebandz joked, getting a few chuckles from the others.

~ ~ ~

About ten minutes later, Mister walked back out of the house and did another quick scan of its surroundings to make sure nothing was out of place. Once satisfied he got in the truck and left, not turning up the radio until he turned onto Mill Road. As he turned into traffic, he relit the blunt he had been smoking before he picked up Endure and unpaused the radio.

Walk across that dirty track

At two o'clock a.m. flat,

Strapped, snatched and dirty gat,

anything move, then murder that

Mister rapped along with Lil' Boosie as he floated down the street on his way to check on the spots before he had to meet back up with Sharky.

Tired of goin' through pressure, man,

'Cuz of that lesson mane,

That shit hit a special vein,

Make you wanna test the 'caine,

I mean if it ain't that dozer or that weed mane,

It's somethin' this solja boy don't need,

'Cuz that 'caine gon' shake you' bread

Mister had just turned on Fond du Lac Avenue

when out of the corner of his eye he saw the screen

of his cellphone lighting up. He scooped it out of the

cup holder and saw missed calls from Sharky and a

text ordering him to call him back ASAP.

"My bad, bro bro, wat it do?" Mister apologized

after muting the radio and calling Sharky back.

"Shit, shit. Where you at, bro?"

"'Bout to get on the Fond du Lac freeway from droppin' off yo' girl. She said she was gon' call you."

"She did. She on the other line. I was a little worried 'cuz neither one of y'all were answering the phone."

"Naw, it's all well. Bro, you know me, I gotta bang these subs. I don't know why you put all this in this bitch when you don't even use it," Mister said, hoping to ease Sharky's mind.

"I bang that shit when I'm taking them long-ass trips, but let me finish holla'n at my bitch. I'ma hit you in a sec. Aye, grab me a couple Red Bulls and some blunts."

"Alright, I got you. In a minute." Mister ended

the call. A short time later, he pulled up and parked

at the gas pump on 60th then ran in the store to get

the things he was asked for. He didn't give the tinted-

up Impala a second glance as it parked at the far

pump.

CHAPTER 7

"Fuck this waiting and following shit, fam. I'm finna snatch this fool now!"

"Alright, Free, fuck it. We can catch him at the pump when he comes back out," Eshy agreed, giving in to the greed and hunger of the others in the car with him. "You and Danny try an' get his ass back in the truck and sway from here without a big-ass scene. Pull over at the first decent spot y'all come to so I can holla at the nigga an' make his ass take us to that loot."

With that said Danny Boy and Freebandz exited the rear of the Impala and split up. Both of them knew what needed to be done, without words. They surrounded Mister, who had his focus on the asses of the two tipsy women as they entered the gas station when he was walking out. He didn't see either one of the two jack boys until they were on him with their guns pressed harshly into his ribs.

"Nigga, don't say shit. Just keep walkin' to the truck!" Freebandz told Mister, pressing his gun in Mister's back to steer him back to the truck.

Mister's first thought was to yell for help from one of the few people that were inside the store, or parked waiting inside vehicles at the pumps. But he looked at the fact that he was being robbed and possibly kidnapped by two plain-faced men with guns and knew it was best to comply if he wanted to live. As soon as the three of them were shielded from clear view between the gas pump and truck, Danny Boy took the keys from him and punched the unlock button on the remote. The sound of the single chirp and flash of the truck lights let them know the alarm system had been disarmed. The big Chevy was a four-door with third-row seating: that's where they made Mister sit so he was easier to control, because there wasn't a way for him to simply jump out and run away from them. The top-to-bottom wall of 15-inch Kicker 9500 subwoofers blocked a rear hatch escape, and the dark limo-tinted windows made it hard for anyone to see what was going down inside the truck.

"Don't be dumb, nigga. Run that shit. Empty all

them pockets. You know how this shit goes!"

"If he don't he gonna learn today!" Danny Boy exclaimed as he quickly pulled away from the gas station. He bent a few corners until he found a nice secluded alley and parked.

The Impala pulled over in front of them, and both Boony and Eshy got out and hurried over to join the bloody interrogation that was going on inside the Tahoe. When they pulled the rear doors open, Mister was pleading with Freebandz not to hit him anymore. Eshy saw that Mister had already been pistol-whipped bloody before he could ask him anything. He hoped he could still think well enough to tell them what they wanted to know.

"Alright, G, that's enough! Let me holla at the

nigga before you kill him with your crazy ass," Eshy

barked from the doorway, making his man stop

hitting Mister instantly. "Now, fam, you see we ain't

finna play with you," he said, and Freebandz slapped

Mister with the gun again to make sure Mister

understood. "I said that's enough, fam. Let me talk

to him! Damn!"

"On the G I'll kill this bitch-ass nigga!"

Freebandz exclaimed, pointing his Glock at the

helpless hostage.

"As you can tell, fam wanna kill somethin', so

let's not play no games." Eshy paused. "Take us to

the stash spot. The real one. We want it all. I know

your man's working with them bricks, and where

there's bricks, there's bandz, so if you wanna live

take us to that shit."

Mister had to think fast. He knew he couldn't take them back to Endure's place, and he wasn't gonna take them to Sharky's main stash house so these fools could rob him blind. But if he didn't give them something, he would be killed.

"Okay, I'll take y'all to it. On my mama I'ma take y'all. Just don't kill me. I ain't shit but a worker; this ain't shit but a worker; this ain't even my truck." He told them, trying to sound as convincing as he could for what he had in mind to work out.

"Fam, we gonna follow y'all. I don't want this bitch-ass nigga bleeding all in my shit," Boony told Danny Boy, who was still behind the wheel of the Tahoe.

Mister gave Danny Boy the directions to a new dope house. He was just about to get the spot up and running for the next evening rush by sending the overflow traffic there from the place they had about a block and a half away.

"Who all in this bitch, nigga?" Freebandz demanded when they stopped in front of the house.

"Ain't nobody in there. On everything, don't too many even know 'bout this spot 'cuz it's where all the re-up at," Mister lied. Danny Boy and Boony went up and knocked on the door to be sure they wouldn't be walking into a trap. When nobody answered they waved to the others to bring Mister up to let them inside. Eshy stayed behind in the Impala to keep watch and so they could get away quickly if they needed to.

Inside the spot Mister gave them what was there, which was only about two and a half ounces of soft brown that was bagged up ready to sell. Danny Boy took over holding Mister at gunpoint, while Freebandz and Boony flipped the house inside out. All they found was a little less than a pound of weed to add to what he had given them.

"I know this ain't it, nigga." Danny Boy whacked him with the gun this time. "Where the cash at? Where's the real stash?"

"It's in the vent next to the door by the bathroom. That's all of it, I swear!" Mister told them, struggling hard not to pass from all of the punishment his head had been taking. His vision was blurry from the blood in his eyes, from the many gashes on his head and face.

Freebandz ran back to the place he was told to look. After a bunch of banging from him kicking to get the vent cover off, he yelled, announcing that he had found it.

"Let's see what we working with," Danny Boy said when Freebandz returned holding a pillowcase.

All that was inside was a large zipper bag of money and about a half a kilo of dope.

"I know this lil shit ain't it, nigga! Where the rest at?" Boony demanded, clearly unhappy with the find.

"That's it. The nigga gone to re-up right now, so that's all that's left."

Freebandz shot Mister in the leg.

"Still think this a game, nigga?" he asked as Mister cried out in pain.

"No, please don't, please don't kill me! That's it! I'm just a worker," he begged from down on the floor, where he fell when he was shot.

"Let's go. This nigga ain't that tough to be lying to us," Danny Boy said, waving the others to follow him out of the house so they could be gone before the police or somebody came to investigate the gunshot.

Freebandz shot Mister in his other leg before running outside and jumping in the Impala, which then stormed off.

CHAPTER 8

Something didn't feel right. Sharky had a bad feeling in his gut because he had been calling Mister over and over for about an hour straight. When he didn't answer, or return any of the calls, Sharky knew there was something wrong. So he activated the GPS friend finder on his cellphone to track him.

"Is everything good, bro?" Zay asked as he rebanded the last five thousand stack of the eighty thousand dollars Sharky just sent with him.

"Man, I don't know. My mans was just on his way here to pick me up, but now his ass way outta the way at one of the spots."

"What, you thinking he there knocking a bitch down or some shit 'cuz he ain't hitting you back?"

"Naw, that fool wouldn't be fuckin' off like that knowing we in the middle of some business. Anyway, he would've told me when we talked." Sharky got a new text, but it wasn't the one he wanted. "Do you think you can run me over them ways so I can see what's up right quick?"

"Yeah, I got you," Zay agreed just as Sky walked in the door from making a run. "You right on time, Sky, 'cuz I need to run him to see what's up with something right quick, and Bear on his way for a split right now."

"Okay, I got this," she said.

"It's already together. Bear should have all the

money for it, but if not still give it to him. I'll get the rest from him later on when I see his good slick-talkin' ass at the bar," Zay told her, grabbing his gun and car keys off the pool table. Then he led Sharky out the door. They got in Zay's Dodge Charger that sat on 24-inch spinners and sped off.

When Zay turned onto the block on 22nd and Starks, the first thing that told Sharky things were all bad was the way his truck was parked carelessly half on the curb. The next thing was finding the front entrance door of the house wide open when they parked.

"What the fuck! This ain't right."

"Yeah, this don't look right," Zay agreed, scanning the surroundings as he drew his gun. "Here, take this and let's go see what's up." He handed Sharky the weapon and retrieved another from its place beneath the driver's seat.

They stalked cautiously up on the porch, and Zay pushed the door open further from his position beside Sharky. Stepping inside the house, they instantly spotted smeared bloody handprints on the wall, and Mister passed out under them. Before Zay could stop him, Sharky rushed to his friends' side.

"Is he alive? Sharky? Is he alive?" Zay inquired as he moved to check the rest of the house to make sure nobody was hiding or dying anywhere else in the place.

"Yeah, barely. Help me get him in the truck so I can take him to the hospital!"

"Naw, Sharky, don't move him! Just call 911 and let 'em come help him."

"This one of my spots," he told him, still kneeling over Mister.

"Man, this was robbery it look like to me. I doubt anything's in this muthafucka. Call 'em and give me that burner so you won't get caught with it. I'ma get gone before them people get here."

"Alright." Sharky did as he was told, passing Zay the gun and calling for an ambulance.

"I'ma hold your pack with me. Just hit me as soon as you can and let me know y'all good. You know the police coming too, bro, 'cuz it's a shooting, right?" Zay pulled the keys from the door lock where they were abandoned and tossed them to Sharky, who waved him off. "Make sho you get at me," he yelled over his shoulder as he jogged back to his car and sped away.

~ ~ ~

As soon as Eshy got them safely to their destination inside of Freebandz's apartment in the projects, they dumped all the stuff they got from the robbery on the coffee table. Boony rolled up some blunts while the others got to counting up the cash that they took from the vent. It ended up being a little over fifty Gs. Eshy took twenty Gs and all the heroin, then let the others bust down the rest.

"Aye, Free, let me get a clean shirt. I got that punk's blood on me and shit," Danny Boy said, stripping down to his wifebeater. "Let me get yours too. Is there some lighter fluid so I can burn this shit? I don't need shit tying us to that house."

"Fam, you act like we just killed a muthafucka. All I did was pop him in the legs. So chill with your scary ass."

"Yeah, okay, I got your scary. Dummy, you think that muthafuka can't die from getting shot in both his legs? You could've hit that main vein and the nigga could bleed to death in like a minute or two. Or could've went into shock and had a heart attack, anything. So I'm being safe."

"Fam, right." Eshy agreed with Danny Boy. "Next time kill a nigga if you gonna shoot him for the hell of it. You should've ended him because he saw y'all's faces a little. What, you don't think he could pick y'all out without hats on? Yeah, y'all burn all that y'all got on."

Freebandz didn't argue because he knew what they were saying was right. He gave Danny Boy a shirt and a pair of black Levis to put on, then took all of the clothes they had on and set them on fire in the firepit in the courtyard before his girlfriend and the kids got home.

The four of them were sitting around talking about all the ways they were going to spend their money, when Danny Boy got the call about Jon, his little brother.

~ ~ ~

A distraught and grieving mother gripped her son's and boyfriends' hands. She squeezed tighter and tighter as they followed a tall slinky Latin man, dressed in a soft gray lab coat, through the busy corridors of the hospital. He was taking them to the sad hospital morgue's viewing room to identify and claim their loved-one's body.

"No, no, wait. I can't do this. I'm not ready to see. Not my baby!" the mother pleaded, frozen in place outside the entrance door of the viewing room. "I can't go in there."

"Okay, Mama, calm down; you don't have to go," Danny Boy said as he held both of his mother's trembling hands and faced her.

"Let us have a minute please," the boyfriend told the lab tech, who seemed to be enjoying the family's pain. "Baby, come sit down for a few so you won't pass out on us, and when you're ready we can go in there," he said as he steered the three of them over to a bank of empty seats.

"Just stay with her out here. I'll do it." Danny Boy volunteered, not liking seeing his mother so distraught. "Mama, I got this; you just sit down," he told her as bravely as he could, unable to hide his pain in his shaky voice.

"I'm sorry, Danny, I can't go through those doors. I thought I could, but now that we here . . . . I . . . I just can't," she explained with fresh tears soaking her chubby cheeks.

Danny Boy could see the sincerity in her eyes as he shook with grief and fear. He knew neither one of them wanted to look at Jon's lifeless body lying on a cold steel table, but he could not leave his little brother in there unclaimed like he didn't have people that loved him. Danny Boy took a deep steadying breath, then stepped inside slowly, behind the creepy lab tech. He stood silently watching as the lab tech folded down the sterile white sheet to unveil Jon's battered face.

"Is this your loved one?"

"Yeah," he confirmed, with a nod and a whisper. Flashes of the laugh they shared the last time they were together popped into Danny Boy's head. "Can I touch him?"

"Sure you can. I ask that you please don't try to move him though," said the tech before walking over to a desk in the corner of the room.

"I won't," Danny Boy promised, stepping closer to stroke Jon's cold face. "I love you, bro, and Mama loves you too. She's here too, but she just can't see you like this. Jonny, whoever did this ain't gonna get away with it. I'ma find 'em, bro, and make 'em hurt," he whispered, allowing a few small tears to escape down his face.

"Excuse me? When you're ready I need you to sign a few forms so an autopsy can be done. It's the law to do one in a murder case. If you don't sign it a judge will order it to be done anyway, and all that would do is delay when the body can release to you and the rest of your family. So it's best just to get it out the way now, so you guys can get the funeral arrangements going and get him put to rest," the lab tech explained, placing a clipboard and pen on the tray table beside the brothers. Danny Boy just silently nodded his head and signed the paper without even looking at the lab tech.

CHAPTER 9

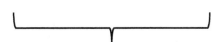

Fame talked on the phone in code so Promiss wouldn't know the type of job assignment he was accepting for the following day. Heavy footed, he unknowingly streaked past a lonely highway patrol car hidden in the dark of an overpass. As soon as Fame confirmed his target and ended the call, a siren blared with bright flashing emergency lights in his rearview mirror. Fame tensed up knowing he was illegal, but pulled to a stop praying the deputy wouldn't want to search the car and would just ticket and release him.

"Shit, I ain't got time for this," he mumbled,

watching the deputy get out of the patrol car. "Aye, Promiss, when he asks you, just tell him we just met today and I'm giving you a ride home, so we can hurry up and get outta here," Fame instructed her without taking his eyes away from the rearview mirror.

"What if he asks where we're coming from?" Promiss asked as she pulled her wallet out of her purse to have her ID card ready.

"Just tell him muthafuckas meet at concerts all the time," he answered, also getting out his driver's license.

"Have you been drinking tonight, or did you just wanna fuck with my peace?" the no-nonsense-looking ginger-haired deputy asked, shinning his Maglite in Fame's face through the open window.

"No, sir, just tryin' to get home," he lied.

"Home, huh? Shut off the engine and step out of the car slowly please?" the deputy ordered, bracing his free hand on his gun.

"Yeah, alright, sir. I got my license in my hand for you, just so you know," Fame informed him as he exited the car, keeping his hands in full view for the deputy.

"Now step to the back of the car and place your hands on the trunk, please!"

Fame handed over his license then walked to the back of his custom-painted wet black-and-gold Honda Accord sitting on 22-inch Monobloc rims like he was told. He watched as the deputy asked Promiss for her ID card while scanning the inside of the car with his flashlight. Promiss passed him the card, and he quickly glanced at it and her before handing it back. He strolled over to Fame and asked him who the woman next to him in the car was.

"A friend," he answered, trying to keep his annoyance in check.

"What's your friend's name?"

"Promiss. I don't know her last name. I just hooked up with her today," he lied again, knowing the deputy was toying with him because he didn't request for him to do a sobriety test, nor did he ask to search the car. "Is something wrong with her?" Fame asked, playing along because at this point in a traffic stop, you're usually either in cuffs or being ticketed.

"Alright." The cop gave Fame a devious grin. "Naw, she's fine. You two be safe and watch your speed on my highway." The deputy handed him back his ID card, releasing him with a warning.

"I will. You have a good night, sir." Fame got back inside and raced away. Checking the rearview he saw the patrol car no longer had on its flashing lights.

"Why were you so nervous, Mr. Man?" asked Promiss as she glanced over her seat and saw the headlights of the patrol car still pacing them a few yards back.

"Because I'm on paper, remember, and I got my gun in here, and this." He pulled out an open bottle of Remy from beneath the seat and took a defiant swig, then offered it to her. "This right here can have me sitting in MSDF on a PO hold for a minute."

"And what about the gun?" She accepted the drink.

"Aww, I ain't worried 'bout him finding it. It's in a safe spot that I can get to when I need to."

"You're bad." She giggled. "I bet he was talkin' shit to you like being the police gives him the right to do whatever the fuck he wanna do to people," she exclaimed, then took a swig from the bottle. Promiss gasped when the liquor hit the back of her throat.

"Whoa, you good." Fame liked the reaction she gave him from the drink, because it told him that she wasn't into hard stuff.

"Man, how do you drink this like that without no soda or nothin'? It taste like gas!" She frowned, passing it back and quickly picking up her water to wash it down.

"Well my pops says I'm an alcoholic, but my mama says he just jealous 'cuz I take after her," he joked. When he glanced her way, he saw her hands wedged between her sexy chocolate thighs as if she was trying to warm them. "You cold?" he asked, already letting up his window.

"You see what I'm wearing, what you think?"

she answered smartly, smiling as he turned on the heater for her.

For their first date after the shooting Promiss had wanted to look extra sexy to him. She dressed scantily in a form-fitting chocolate leather and cream-colored Christian Louboutin miniskirt, with a matching baby doll top. Promiss hoped to seduce Fame into another round of hot sex that didn't end in her sneaking out on him.

"Naw, I'm driving, so I can't see it. Smart ass." He smiled. "Why don't you take it off so I can get a good look at it?" Fame dared with a wink.

"Oooh, you know what!" She slapped him on the shoulder and took the bottle from him, then had another drink from it to give her the courage to let go and get wild with him. "Is that what you want? Do you really wanna see me?" asked Promiss, taking another sip from the bottle. She then slid her skirt up and flirtatiously wiggled out of her little black lace panties. She waved them in front of him, then dropped them in his lap. "How about that?"

"Girl, what you doing?" He picked up the panties, grinning with surprise and a bit of lust in his eyes. "I'm driving and I see you trying to get it poppin'," he said, glancing down at her pretty shaved peach that instantly had his length fully awake.

"I'm just helping you to see me so you can keep your eyes on the road." She hesitated for a moment, wondering how far she should go with her tease. Mind made up, she started rubbing her mound while at the same time popping the buttons of her shirt. "Are you ready for the rest?" she asked, teasing her tight nipples and giving Fame a sexy side-eye view.

"Promiss, I'm driving, and you know I just took

a job up in Minnesota that I gotta be at first thing in the morning," said Fame, fighting to keep an eye open on the busy road.

"Now what that gotta do with anything?" She was feeling a little tipsy now, and a lot more hot.

"I'm just saying, as much as I want to, I can't spend the night with you 'cuz I gotta get on the road right away in a couple hours."

"Shut up and stop making excuses. Just find a spot someplace to park. I don't need you to spend the night, I need to be fucked. I wanna feel you in me right now," she told him, while rubbing his erection through his jeans with one hand and working herself a little more with the other.

Fame was too turned on to say anything. When he merged to get off at the next exit, Promiss took his hand and slid it across her warm thigh. She spread her legs wider, allowing his thick fingers to touch her clit. He made it up the exit ramp while at the same time teasing her button the way she encouraged him to. She hummed and moaned out her pleasure as her wetness coated his fingers, and he repeatedly dipped them in and out of her warmth. Promiss had her hand fishing inside his zipper, fighting to get to what she wanted as he worked her until she grew to the point of release. She almost growled when she pulled his hand away and put his fingers in her mouth, unable to stop from cumming on his soft leather seat. As soon as Fame threw the car in park she had his length free and in her warm mouth.

"Hmm, shit, girl!" he groaned, welcoming her mouth work, laying his head back on the headrest. "Woo, stop, hold up. Get in the back so I can give you what you really need." He kissed her before she climbed over the seat.

Fame had to get out of the car and back in to join her without breaking either of the 12-inch screens he embedded in the headrest while trying to get his big body between her legs. As soon as the door closed and locked behind him, he had a nipple between his lips. Using the tip of his hardness, he played with her clit a few hot seconds before ramming it deep inside her.

"Yesss, babe, yes!" Promiss cried, lost in pure ecstasy. "Get this pussy! Harder, hummm, harder!"

Fame's rhythm increased as he pounded harder and deeper, causing Promiss to get louder, not caring who heard them. Soon he felt her wetness clenching and legs shaking. She felt so good cumming that he busted right behind her, locked in each other's arms.

"I love you!" Promiss whispered as they kissed.

~ ~ ~

Slim strolled out of his apartment on East Ruby Street dressed in his signature black hoody, backpack, and loose-fit Dickie's jeans. When he made it over to Fame, who was leaning on the car looking worn down, he had to think fast as Fame tossed him the keys to the trusty, inconspicuous Buick.

"You drive, I'm tired as fuck, bro," Fame admitted, climbing into the passenger's seat.

"Something told me I was gonna have to drive." Slim got in, started the car, and pulled off. "You got it bad, man. Ole girl gotta have some fire-ass pussy to have you all late and lazy and shit."

"Dawg, don't worry 'bout how good my bitch's pussy is. That ain't the only reason I'm late."

"But it is a part of it. Did you run out on her this

time, or did she use you again?" Slim asked jokingly.

"Naw, I beat that pussy in the back seat of my whip parked on a side street. I had her screaming she love me an' shit," Fame boasted as he retrieved the down payment for the murder they were headed to commit. "I'm late because I had to wait for this." He waved the rubber-banded stack of bills in Slim's face.

"Is it all there, 'cuz that looks light."

"This is half, but I ain't count it yet. The muthafucka ain't stupid. He know how we get down, so he ain't gon' take a chance cheating us."

"Okay, count that shit later and just take your ass to sleep 'cuz I'ma need you to tell me how to get to the spot from St. Paul," Slim said, getting right on the freeway, headed toward Minnesota.

Four lonely hours later, Slim started to fray from

being bored and hearing Fame softly snoring, out cold in the seat beside him. He toyed with the power of the Buick, making a mental note to get the oil changed when they made it back to Milwaukee, and no matter what Fame said, he planned to put a better radio in the car as well, because of long trips like this, where all that is on is rock, country, and static for him to listen to.

"Fame! Fame! Fame?" he chanted as soon as they crossed the state line. "Wake up! Good snoring-ass nigga!"

"Whu? What up?" Fame questioned, slowly pulling himself out of dreamland.

"We're here in Minnesota."

"I thought you was gonna wake me up when we got to St. Paul. What happened to that?" he asked when he looked out the window and saw nothing but empty land, trees, and farm animals.

"I couldn't take no more of your snoring. You sound like a chainsaw massacrer locked in a closet."

"No I don't. Fuck you!"

They laughed, and the static instantly cleared up on the radio, giving them a hot morning mix to jam to. It was a sure sign you were in eastern Minnesota when you got 101.3 out of the Twin Cities. They rolled the rest of the way to the motel not far from the interstate, which was where their target would be late in the morning. All they had to do was wait.

CHAPTER 10

About 5:00 a.m., the talk of the young thug's murder was all over social media. In all of what was being posted, no one had any useful accounts about the day of the kidnapping and murder that could help Danny Boy catch up with his brother's killers. Danny Boy was unable to sleep because of his loss. Him and Jon were three years apart but had a very close and loving relationship. All sleeping did for him was increase the heartbreak, so Danny Boy drank and smoked, trying to find and escape from himself, because dealing with all of the self-ridicule and anger was impossible. It was so hard for him to fathom that

just the other day Jon was having breakfast with him

and their mother, talking about school, and getting

along better with their stepfather. Now he was about

to commit an armed robbery just to help pay for his

baby brother's extravagant funeral arrangements.

"What it do, fam!" greeted Freebandz, sliding

into the passenger's seat of his dead homie's car. "Do

you really think we should be making this move in

this area, fam?" he inquired, removing his gun from

his waist to get comfortable.

"Free, if you on that same shit Eshy on, then you

can take yo' ass back to the crib. That go for you too,

Boony!" Danny Boy snapped, not looking at either

one of them. "I'm doing this for my brother, and I

want all you muthafuckas to know it, so hell yeah

I'ma drive his whip."

"DB, chill. You way too hot mouthed right now,

fam. We got love for Jon G too. We got our ear to the streets hunting the muthafuckas that took his life too," said Boony from the backseat.

"Yeah, nigga, so if you wanna take lil fam's spirit with us by driving his car to get that bread to send him home like a real G, then say no mo' and let's go," Freebandz added, looking into Danny Boy's misery-filled eyes.

Both men knew Danny Boy needed to go in this move for more reasons than just because he needed the cash. He also had a lot of emotions to work through, and for thugs like them it's sometimes better to cause pain than to face their own.

"Aye, Lil Gabar wanna go in this move with us, and I think we gon' need him," Boony told Danny Boy. "I already told him it was cool."

"Okay, his punk ass should be here since he

wasn't nowhere around when my brother needed his ass the most," he agreed harshly as he drove out of the parking lot of the Park Lawn housing projects.

After Boony ended his call letting Gabar know they were on the way to pick him up, Danny Boy unpaused his brother's mixtape. The car vibrated from the heavy bass of the last song Jon had recorded.

When I touch down,

I'ma need a fat package of hard,

'Cuz I'ma hustle 'til I got it,

Or I'm back on the yard,

I know how it is to be reliant on fam,

To be honest fam,

I rather just rely on the yam.

My advice to y'all suckas is to stay non-existent,

'Cuz fam I'ma keep my distance,

So, when y'all fall on ya faces,

Don't expect my assistance

They all rapped along as Danny Boy whipped the black Mercury Marquis across town towards a small credit union on the city's north-west side. This cash store was the spot the four diabolical thugs intended to stick up on the extremely misty morning.

Fam told me actions speak louder,

and words will have a thug riding stiff in a

hearse, So when it's time to get my hands dirty,

I don't play in the dirt

They arrived just in time to witness the familiar black Chevy Caprice pull into the credit union's parking lot and sit waiting in the corner of the lot with nothing but its fog lights on, the way it had on all of the days they had watched it before.

"There he go, right on time!" Boony pointed out

excitedly.

"Yeah, I see. I'ma pull around the other side so you and Gabar can get out and—"

"Fuck that, he just sitting his fat lazy ass there chillin'. Pull up next to him, or better yet, block his ass in and let's make his ass get in the trunk," Freebandz suggested, read to move.

"Let's do it," Danny Boy agreed even though that wasn't the way they had planned this robbery to go.

Before the Mercury came to a complete stop, Freebandz and Gabar jumped out. Gabar fired a warning shot through the guard's windshield as Freebandz and Boony ran up on the driver's door. Boony easily smashed the window with the butt of the big Highpoint .45 automatic.

"Pop the fuckin' trunk!" Boony ordered. When the stunned guard didn't move, he hit him in the face with the gun, breaking the man's nose. "I said pop the muthafuckin' trunk, bitch, or I pull the trigger and do it my damn self!"

This time the dazed guard did as he was told. While Boony snatched the gun off the guards, him and Garber climbed in the car from the passenger's side, doing a quick search for any more weapons. The guard didn't understand why he was being assaulted, but thought as long as he cooperated, he would be able to get out of the trunk and run for help. Little did he know, Danny Boy had a thirst for blood. He shot the poor guard in the face, then slammed the trunk shut. They scanned their surroundings to make sure there weren't any witnesses.

Freebandz voluntarily put on the guard's hat and uniform jacket and sat behind the wheel of the Caprice. He knew Danny Boy was mad at Garber for the hole he shot in the windshield, and didn't want to make a scene. As soon as Danny Boy and the others parked the Marquis on the other end of the parking lot, the manager's red Saturn Vue turned into the lot right on time and parked in the reserved space.

Freebandz tapped the horn two short rapid times, the way he witnessed the real guard do many times before. So he guessed it was some kind of code they had. Then he got out and met up with the man on his way to the side door of the building, just as he'd seen the guard do.

"Good morning!"

"Morning. I wish I could've stayed my ass at home today."

"Me too. This that good sleeping weather right here. I almost didn't answer my phone when they called me in."

"Dave must have gotten lucky with that girl he's been talking about lately, huh?"

"I don't know, Dave. I haven't been working for this company long," Freebandz lied, walking and making small talk with the trusting manager. As soon as he unlocked the door and punched in the cash store's disarm code on the keypad on the inside wall beside the door, Freebandz pressed his gun to the man's head. "Keep your hands at your side where I can see 'em!" he ordered, then snatched the panic button from around the manager's neck and pushed the door open for Danny Boy and Gabar to enter.

"Alright, alright! You know what we here for. Don't try no funny shit and you will make it home at the end."

Everyone except the manager knew that wasn't true by the way Danny Boy did the guard. They gathered up everything of value they could find: money, coins, postage stamps, bus passes, and even a currency counter. After forcing the manager to give them all of the video, Danny Boy shot him twice in the chest like they knew he would. Then they quickly fled the building. They all had on latex gloves, so they weren't worried about leaving fingerprints.

"Gabar, you drive the Caprice so it won't bring attention to the place too fast. I'ma ride with you. Boony, y'all follow us," Ordered Danny Boy.

Gabar should've known something wasn't right about this, but he wanted to prove himself to Danny Boy and make him forgive him for running off on Jon the day he was kidnapped and killed. Danny Boy got the guard's gun from Freebandz, then followed Gabar over to the Caprice. He waited until the young fool sat behind the wheel, then put the Glock .40 to

ASSA RAYMOND BAKER

Gabar's temple.

"Fuck you, you soft-ass bitch! My brother might be here if it wasn't for you!" he snapped, then squeezed the trigger a few times before Gabar could make any excuses.

Even though he knew there was no one to stop Gabar's execution, Danny Boy dropped the gun beside the car and jogged over and jumped in the backseat of Jon's Marquis, fired up and ready to continue bringing justice to those who had any hand in his little brother's death. Boony nonchalantly drove away, shaking his head at what he had just witnessed.

CHAPTER 11

It was sometime after ten o'clock in the morning,
and so far, the only thing the death-dealing thugs had
done was eat and window shop. They were
camouflaged in a herd of people inside Minnesota's
amazing Mall of America, observing their target and
his friends' every move. Fame and Slim didn't know
the relationship of the man and women he was
traveling with, but they wished they would go home
or someplace so they could get the job done.

Fame learned that the man him and Slim took the
hit on was so very gay. He was told that the guy
managed to be manipulated over a hundred thousand

dollars in cash, and another two-hundred thousand or so in jewelry from the mother of the very powerful Chicago gang leader. It didn't matter to them that their target was gay, but it did make them wonder if the story they had been fed was true; because from what they could see there wasn't anything about the man that said he was straight.

After following him for another ninety minutes, Slim got a fiendish idea that played on their target's sexuality. His plan would only work if his rugged good looks made him the man's type. If not, the promise of sex always worked. Playing the part would be easy for the undercover bi-sexual thug. His only issue was getting up the nerve to run the plan by his partner and good friend.

"Bro, we need to get this lame someplace alone so we can handle our business and get back to the

Mil' before it gets late."

"Let me find out you missing your lil sweet Promiss," Slim teased.

"Dawg, you sound like you're jealous. I'ma tell her to plug you with one of her buddies so you can shut the fuck up."

I'ma hold you to that, but I think I can get 'em to leave, or at least break away from the others for a few, but you gotta fall back and let me work."

"If what you got in mind will speed this shit up, I'm with it."

On that note, Slim broke away from Fame, leaving him alone to continue following the target while he went shopping. After hitting two stores, Slim went into the nearest restroom to freshen up and change into the outfit he thought would best catch the man's attention.

"Bro, you sure you ain't did this before?" Fame inquired when Slim rejoined him, dressed in a lazy two-toned brown Ermenegildo Zegna lightweight sweater, black fitted pants, and soft brown Christian Louboutin boots. "Bro, I ain't never seen you dress up like this for a female. Let me find out!"

"Miss me with that, Fame. I'm taking one for the team so I can get you back to wifey."

"Go do your thang, bro. You know how it go. What happens in the Mall of America, stays in the Mall of America."

They laughed and followed the target and his friends up to the lounge that was on the upper level of the very crowded mall. When the two assassins stepped off the elevator behind the trio, they parted ways. Fame fell back so Slim could be seen entering the place alone, but he wasn't far behind.

Before he crossed the threshold Slim knew he was a bit overdressed for the simple place, but that was all part of his game of seduction. People in places like this always get curious and want to know what's up with an expensively dressed mysterious type. Slim played the role well, choosing to sit in the middle of the row of empty stools at the bar. He ordered a vodka and iced Red Bull as soon as the David Spade-looking bartender made himself available to him. Slim gulped down the vodka and cooled his throat with the Red Bull chaser after tactfully waiting until the bartender returned his attention to the greenish-tinted dark-haired women and friends he was talking with before having to do his job. Slim pretended to flag down the chatty bartender while making flirtatious eye contact with his mark, who was sitting not far from the bartender at the far end of the bar.

The target got the bartender's attention before getting up and excusing himself from the coupled he had been venturing through the city and mall with all day. Slim stopped staring, cocky that things were going as planned. He nonchalantly scanned the place, looking for Fame, who he knew without a doubt was watching his back.

"I got this round for sure. Now if you allow me to join you, the drinks are on me for as long as you're here," the mark said to Slim, timing his sudden interruption perfectly with the bartender placing two fresh drinks in front of them.

"Thanks for the refill. As you see, there are plenty of open seats for you to help yourself to," Slim replied, looking him up and down now that he was sitting beside him. Slim had to admit to himself that if this was another time the mark could definitely get some playtime. "Tell me, do I look like I can't afford to buy my own drinks?"

"No, you actually look too good to have to. You look like the type that's used to paying for everything for everyone all the time. Am I close?" he asked with a smooth, confident tone.

"You're not far off."

"I guessed as much. So let me be the one who treats you right for a change. I know you've been told that it's never good to drink alone."

"How can I turn that down?" Slim grinned, picking up his vodka. "A, I'm not drinking alone. Can you not see the size of the crowd in here?" He gulped the shot, then asked if the couple that he saw him with would be joining them.

"Umm, nooo. I came over here because I've had

enough of my sister and her guy for now. Anyway, they're where they want to be; they're here visiting the mall more than they are me." He chuckled.

"I take it it's their first time here? Where are they from, if it's not a secret?"

"Oh, no secrets here." The mark grinned. "They're up from Raine in Wisconsin. What about you, where you from?"

"Just outside of Madison, Wisconsin. Like you're doing now, I'm taking a break from visiting with family, and like your sister and her guy, it's my first time visiting the mall. It's the amusement park that gets us." Slim smiled. "Did anyone ever tell you that you kinda look like the actor Chris Pine?"

"No, but if he's the type you're into, I'll take it," he flirted.

"Okay, Chris, my name's Tim Driver, but

everyone calls me Driver," Slim lied, extending his hand.

"Mine is actually Chris. That's why I laughed when you said it," he lied, in full con-man mode as he held Slim's hand a few moments longer after their handshake.

"Now that we're friends and if you really wanna be nice to me, why don't we get outta here?" Slim suggested, and watched his smile widen.

"Can you give me a moment to let my sister know?"

"Sure, I'd think less of you if you didn't. I'ma hit the head right quick, and I'm ready if you are."

When Slim slid off of the stool and started walking away from the target, Fame made himself visible to his partner. At the same time, he kept his eyes on Chris, who was now back with the couple

Fame wanted to get him away from. Frustrated, Fame looked over to Slim, weaving through dancers and tables. That's when he saw Slim signaling him to meet him in the restroom. As they passed each other once there, Slim explained to him that he had convinced the mark to leave with him.

"I don't know what he's telling them two he's with, or how good of a look they got of my face. So if he gets shot, they gon' have the law at my head."

"Don't trip, bro. I'ma literally save that ass," Fame joked.

"I'ma text you when I'm ready, but you need to hit me back and let me know that exit y'all gonna come out of. Mr. Shiesty is about to be a victim of a deadly hit-and-run. With his ole extra-freaky ass," he joked, before leaving to find an easy car to steal.

Close to fifteen minutes or so later, Fame was

sitting double-parked outside of the exit that Slim had texted him. Slim waited in the clean white Cadillac Deville he had swiped from an employee's reserved parking spot on the west side of the huge mall. Engine idling, he received another text telling him they would be walking out in about two minutes. He moved the Caddy into the best position to get this job over with.

As soon as Fam spotted them walking out of the building, he sent Slim a text telling him to get out of the way. Slim fell back, pretending to be on an important call with his job.

"You take care of that; I'll get my car," the target said, then continued heading toward his shiny gray Mercedes-Benz.

When shiesty Chris Pine was far enough away from Slim, Fame stomped the gas pedal to the floor, and the Caddy shot off like a bullet.

The Caddy slammed into the man at full speed, sending him flying backward. When his body crashed to the ground in an awkward, bloody mess, Fam ran it over just to make sure the job was done. The breaks went out all of a sudden, causing Fame to have no other choice but to crash it into the wall in from of him. His head slammed into the steering wheel on the Caddy's impact. Dazed, but aware that he needed to get out of the stolen wreck, and far away from it fast, he dragged himself out of the car just as Slim pulled up in their trusty Buick. Fame opened the rear door and dove onto the back seat as Slim sped away before the helpful mall-goers knew what all was going on.

CHAPTER 12

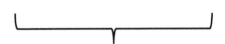

TGIF! Everyone in the city seemed to be rushing to get ready for their weekend. Almost all of the car washes and beauty shops were packed with people, full of anticipation and with cash burning a hole in their pockets. It seemed like the entire city of Milwaukee was out in traffic. Usually on days like this Danny Boy and his team of sadistic marauders would have been hard at work trying to rob as many nouns as they could. But after Credit Union and Von's funeral, Eshy suggested they all lay low for a while.

"Come on, DB, come out and kick it with us.

Forever's gonna be there and you know she trying to get up with you," Summer schemed, trying hard to convince Danny Boy to go out to the club with them.

"Yeah?" He perked up at the thought of finally hooking up with her super-fine stripper friend.

"Yeah, fam, its's true. The bitch took off work just to fuck with you. You know it's time to get out and get back to living yo' life, fam, cuz right now from what we're all seeing, you ain't living, my nigga," Freebandz added.

"Free, y'all ain't even like that. I just ain't feelin' it tonight. I'm trying to chill and binge watch *24*."

"DB, if you don't come out with us, then we're stuck with you, 'cuz mama got the kids, I ain't tryna be in the house, and Free still got the car in the shop," Summer listed.

"Well there you go. You heard her, fam, you got two choices here in front of you. One, go home, get dressed, and go with us, or we all go to your crib and binge-watch Jack save the world one day at a time together. So, what you finna do?" Freebandz pressed.

"You two muthafuckas ain't as smart as you think. You know me, Free. There's always another choice." Danny Boy grinned wickedly as he headed toward his house instead of dropping them off at theirs like he was doing first. "I can have my alone time and just give y'all the car for the night. I don't need it, and if I do decide to go out, I got the Marques. So now the choice is on y'all. Do you wanna use the car and go kick it, or walk home with all them bags you got from my crib?" he asked, pulling over in front of his house. "Cuz I'm chillin."

"Okay give us the car," Freebandz answered,

sounding defeated. He slid over into the driver's seat when Danny Boy got out of the car.

"So what about Forever? You had me doing all that talking to her for you, and when she gives in you stand her up. What typa shit is that?" Summer exclaimed, still trying to persuade him to stop sitting in the house grieving constantly.

"Summer, it ain't. Let her know that I ain't on no tit-for-tat shit with her. I just really don't wanna be around no big-ass crowds right now. I just got done dealing with all of my family. The last of them just went back down South this morning, so I just need to relax and chill. Tell her I said that ass too phat to give up on, and I'm back at it when things are less intense for me."

"Okay, but All-Stars is finna be all the way live tonight, and this might be the last chance you get to watch Forever twerk it for you for free," Summer said, trying one last time to persuade him from his extenuating period of lonely mourning.

"Y'all have fun. My phone will be on, so call me if you need me. Fam, tell that nigga Boony not to get on that drunk shit tonight, cuz I ain't got it to bail nobody out of jail," Danny Boy said before heading inside the house for the night.

~ ~ ~

"So he at home right now?" Forever inquired when she got with Summer before they headed out to All-Stars Night Club.

"Yep, we just left him," she answered, fixing her own makeup in the mirror of her small Parklawn bathroom.

"You left him by himself, because he don't need to be alone after just losing his lil-brother like that."

"Yep, he said he didn't feel like being around no crowds. I tried telling him it's not good to be by himself like that, but he ain't hear me though."

"Hey, can y'all take me to pick up some food and drop me off at his crib? He said that he didn't want to be around no crowds, and I'm not that. I really don't wanna be all out like that tonight anyways."

"Hell yeah, I got you, bitch, as long as you do my nigga right."

"Free, would you go some damn where, dipping in our business an' shit!" Summer retorted over her shoulder at her man, who was laughing as he went down the steps. She saw that Freebandz had a lil blunt between his fingers and hated that she let him leave with it.

When the women were done with their lengthy beautification processes, they collected Freebandz from in front of the TV playing *Call of Duty*, then headed out for the night. It was maybe an hour and a half later from when Forever had decided she was going to drop in on Danny Boy unannounced, that she was standing on his porch. This was her first time at his home, so she both knocked and pressed the doorbell just in case it didn't work.

"What up, girl! Why you here?" Danny Boy asked once he opened the door.

"Well hey to you too. I thought you would've been more happy to see me standing here," she flirted, spotting the sadness in his deep brown eyes.

"Did they tell you I'm not in the mood for y'all games? Now, bye!" he said with a harshness to his voice that she kind of found sexy.

"No! DB, wait," she shouted stepping forward as he was about to shut the door in her face. The current irritation showing in his face did not change the fact that seeing him emotional and raw like this was a turn-on for her. "I'm not here to play, if you don't wanna play, but I had them drop me off over here, so you can't just leave me out here like this, Danny. I'm here cuz I wanna be here, for real. Look, I brought us something to eat and drink." She held up the bag.

"Let me be your someone to talk to or do whatever with. Let me be here for you tonight?"

Danny Boy was so surprised to see Forever standing on his porch, that he did not notice the two bags dangling from her hands until she said something about bringing food. He did a quick scan of the block to see if she really had them leave her there. He didn't find any sign of them or any cars that did not belong there.

He shook his head and stepped aside.

"Come in, but don't think I couldn't have left your ass sitting out here on the porch until you had somebody come get you."

"I know you wouldn't have left me out there, because you didn't," she retorted once inside. "But I'm sorry for real if I did interrupt you doing something important," she apologized, looking around. "I came here because I'm in the mood for something different tonight. I work in clubs all the damn time, so I already know what I'm not missing there. But I don't know what's going on with you. To be real with you, DB, I was only going to All-Stars tonight because of you," she confessed.

Forever had plans on getting him deep between her luscious legs and doing all the things she knew would make him forget his grief for a little while. From the way he was ogling her figure, she knew it was not going to be hard. Forever was dressed to tease wearing a fitted gold silk button-up blouse that stopped just before her waist, snug-fitting signature Dolce & Gabbana leggings and gold crystal red bottom pumps.

"What's in them bags smellin' so good?" he asked, plucking them from her and placing them on the blue-tinted glass coffee table. "I was just trying to think of something to order me to eat when you came," he told her, pulling containers out of the bags and setting them on the table.

"I hope you like Chinese food and soda, cuz that was all I could think of that wasn't out of the way of the club and that wouldn't take long to pick up."

"What! Girl, Chinese is one of my favorite foods. Please tell me you got both beef and shrimp fried rice?" He opened one of the containers before she could answer. "What's this?"

"Pepper steak and gravy. You can put that down cuz that's my favorite. You know what, I'ma share it with you since I didn't get your beef fried rice." She got out a black plastic fork, dipped it in the container, and then fed him a thick piece of meat dripping with brown sauce. "Do you like it?"

"It's good, yeah, I like it. I wouldn't let it go to waste knowing how hard you work for your money." He then took a chance, tapping her on her butt.

"Danny, don't start nothing you ain't ready to finish, now." She smiled, then proceeded to prepare paper plates of the food for the two of them. She then retrieved two 20-ounce Faygo sodas from the bag. "Which one you want, orange or grape?"

"Why is it only orange or grape for me? What's up with that cream joint I seen in there?" He tested, already knowing that she loved cream soda from the numerous times that he'd seen her with one in the past.

" Aww, man, I like you, but I can't give that up."

"I'm just fucking with you. I know you drink those all the time. I always see you with 'em when you be at fam 'nem's crib." He eased her mind all the way about the drink by plucking the orange one from her hand.

"Danny, do you like 'em for real?"

"Yep, but I love me some orange."

They continued to chat about everything but his brother's murder, which Forever did not mind doing because it meant she was giving his mind and heart a break from the pain of it. They really got to know a lot about each other as they ate. She found out that he had not been trying to hook up with her just for the fantasy of being with a stripper. Forever felt like he really liked her, which turned her on even more.

When they were done eating, Danny Boy was glad that she had popped up the way she had. He really did need the intimacy. It took his mind off of all that was going on with him and his family. Even though his mother said she didn't blame him for what happen to her baby, he still felt awful for still not knowing who did it.

"Why is it so quiet in here? Turn on some music," she suggested, then fell back lazily on the couch. Forever unsnapped a few buttons on her top. "Oooh, turn on something mellow we can chill to if you got something mellow in your playlist."

Danny Boy did not feel like searching for a good list on his brother's iPod that sat in the cradle where he had put it the last time he was over at the house.

So Danny Boy just turned on the radio and put it on 98.7 FM and was rewarded with the smooth old-school sound of Jodeci's hit song "Feenin'."

Take my money

My house and my car

For one hit of you

You can have it all, baby

Danny Boy strolled back over to Forever and boldly reach down and finished unbuttoning her shirt. He found instantly found out that she was not wearing a bra. He eagerly pulled the top all the way off of her. The sight of her perky nipples made his mouth water for a taste of her.

Cuz makin' love

Every time we do

Girl, it's worse than drugs

Cuz I'm an addict over you

And you know that I

I can't leave you alone

Forever submitted all the way into the moment by clasping his hand and placing it over her breast. From his skin touching hers, a low lusty breath escaped her. She loved the simple feeling of his warm touch. She tugged him close and kissed him. Danny Boy parted his lips accepting her tongue returning the kiss, with a hunger of his own. Forever slid beneath him without breaking their lip lock, then slowly worked his shirt off over his head. She smiled, liking the scenery of his solid heavily tattooed chest and shoulders. One displaying an angel battling a demon, the words *Ihdinas siratal Mustaaqeem* running across his upper chest, and the other shoulder had the hand of God reaching down from the clouds. Forever dragged her hand down his firm abs and shuddered with anticipation.

I can't leave you alone

You got me feenin'

(Got me going crazy)

I can't leave you alone

You got me feenin' for you

Danny Boy kissed his way down her neck. When his lips touched her nipples, she got even wetter. He moved masterfully back and forth between her nipples as she went to work wiggling out of the leggings.

Forever was not wearing any panties. With the thin barrier off she unfastened and shoved down his jeans and boxers in one go, freeing his thick erection. The sex kitten purred when he dragged it up and down between her split three times nice and slow teasingly before pushing it inside of her. He went right to work, pounding her warm wet box hard and fast for a full two minutes. Then he suddenly slowed to a stop.

"I need you to let it all out, Danny. Fuck me hard; cum for me, daddy. We got all night," she promised then began slowly rotating her wide hips, holding him deep in her by his butt cheeks as they kissed.

He groaned, fighting not to cum first. He could no longer take just letting her work and began stroking her long and slow, making sure she felt every one of his hard ten inches. She clenched her silk-soaked muscles around his thickness as she continued to grind with him. She matched him until he picked up the pace. As soon as he changed speeds, she squirted her first wave of the big orgasm that was building up for a tidal-wave release.

Danny Boy could not hold back once he felt her light spray. It felt so good. He growled, pulling out to release warm cum on her belly. Forever was not done with him. She took hold of his length and milked it good before pushing it back inside of her. He was instantly hard all over again from the way her wetness squeezed him, pulsating as she came loudly.

A minute or two later Danny Boy pulled out of her again. Only this time it was to flip her over on all fours so he could punish it from the back. But before he dove back in, he dropped to his knees and licked her split and sucked on her clit from beneath her. He gripped her ass with his rough hands to ensure she did not pull away.

They were just catching their second winds when someone started banging recklessly on the exterior door like they were the police.

"Nooo, who the fuck is that, Danny? It better not be the next bitch!" she warned him as she climbed off of his wet face.

"It ain't no other bitch. I don't know who the fuck

it is." He pulled on his pants and slipped into his

shoes before marching over and snatching the door

open in anger. "Who the fuck—"

CHAPTER 13

"**Danny Mays?**" **an MPD officer inquired with** his weapon drawn hanging at his side. "I got a warrant for you arrest!"

"What?" Danny exclaimed, stepping back. "For what? I ain't did shit!"

"Calm down, sir, and keep your hands where I can see them!" the officer ordered, pushing his way into the house along with three others.

"What's going on?" Forever demanded, pulling her shirt on to cover up some.

"I don't fuckin know what this is about. You muthafuckas see I'm with my girl, and we've been here all night!" Danny Boy fussed.

"Miss, could you put some pants on or cover yourself better please?" a poker-faced female officer told Forever when she noticed her teammates were ogling the other women's nude lower half.

"How about you tell us why you in here?"

"Forever, just do what they tell you!" Danny Boy told her, making her check herself. "And get my phone and call my moms so she knows what's going on," he said, then addressed the officer that held him at gunpoint. "Can I put on my shirt right here before we go since y'all ain't telling me shit before I go to jail?"

The officer standing the closest to the shirt picked it up and tossed it to him. Forever watched Danny Boy dress in the shirt then watched the officer roughly slap the cold steel handcuffs tightly on his wrists before they promptly marched him outside. She followed them promising Danny Boy she would make sure everyone knew where he was. Then the officer stuffed him into the back of a squad car.

Everything seemed to be moving like a dream as she stood on the porch watching the four officers pile back into the two cars and speed away from the house. Forever continued to watch their bright lights flashing silently as they vanished from sight. Then she went back inside and found his phone as well as her own. She found that both of them had a multitude of missed calls and text messages. Forever quickly went through Danny Boy's contact list and called his mother like she was told. Then she replied to the texts on her phone that she had from Summer, telling her to come over to Danny Boy's house ASAP.

~ ~ ~

All the way to the police station Danny Boy racked his brain trying to put two and two together as to what they had taken him in for. He could not think of anything that would help him better prepare himself for whatever was to come. The thug knew how careful he always was not to leave any real evidence behind that could link him to any of the many crimes he had been involved in. All he could do was shake his head in disgust for being in back of the squad car. He just stared at his arresting officer's head through the shatterproof glass partition.

"Aye, I know y'all know exactly what you muthafuckas got me in here for! And you gotta tell me cuz if not then this shit is kidnapping!" he yelled at them just to express his anger.

"Just because you think you know my job so

well, here's a hint for you. You should be thinking of names for your grandchildren right now, and if you don't have any kids you never will, punk. Now shut the hell up, before I have my partner make a stop in an alley!" the officer barked at him.

The thug smiled but did not say another word. Once they were at the 5th District police station he was immediately taken from the car and placed in back of a paddy-wagon for transport to county. The wagon was crowded with a bunch of funky homeless-looking people. All he could do was hope that Forever did like he asked her and that she was truly the person he felt that he made a real connection with, and not just another gold digger that many of his guys said she was.

No one told Danny Boy what he was locked up for until he was inside the Milwaukee County jail's booking room.

"Mays! Do you know what you're being charged with?" asked the desk sergeant as he began the booking process.

"No, ain't nobody told me nothing," he answered nervously.

"Really? Okay, you are being charged with attempted first-degree reckless homicide, for the beating that you and your friends put on that poor guy. A poor guy who was just out trying to have a good time with his girl."

"Man, I don't know what in the fuck you are talking about. I was at home with my girl all night. Fuck that. I ain't got shit to say else. Not until I talk to a lawyer."

With that said, he was booked and placed in the waiting area with a phone that was out of order. The remaining hours of the night dragged on by. Once he was put in a cell on the receiving unit, Danny Boy would have thought he was in a bad dream if not for the scent of the sex he had with Forever on his skin.

"I can't leave you alooooone. You got me feenin. Feenin for yooou!" he sang out loud, then laughed at it, locked in the lonely cell just reminiscing on how good she felt.

CHAPTER 14

Early Saturday morning before beginning their workday, Promiss, Endure, and Shay sat across from one another listening as Shay told them about the bloody brawl she witnessed at All-Stars the night before. Promiss had been awakened by the tintinnabulation of her phone from the social media post of it, but it was nothing like hearing it from a drama queen like her cousin.

"I know y'all heard about that big-ass fight at the club," Shay started. "It's all everybody was posting about."

"Yeah, I seen that. Was you there?" Endure asked

between sips of her blended French vanilla cappuccino.

"Bitch, you know I was. I was trying to catch me something warm and strong to bounce up and down on for the night." She snickered. "But what they ain't sayin on the book is that ole wretched-ass bitch Summer started the shit," Shay told them.

"Summer?" Promiss repeated with a frown. "Where do I know that name from?"

"Promiss, she that sleazy skinny stripper bitch that broke out all of Mercy Bondz's wife's car windows last year after his wife beat her ass for stealing from her fine-ass kickboxer son," Endure reminded her.

"Yep, that's that hoe. She got her ass beat again last night, too, by this girl named China for doing some more foul shit."

"Shay, I thought it was a bunch of dudes fighting last night?" Endure inquired, trying to get the story straight.

"It was, but they were too. It was two fights at the same time. A good-ass Royal Rumble in that bitch! This dude name Asad had checked Summer for something. I don't know what the bitch said, but that's when her and China started having words. So Asad got between them. I guess he was trying to defuse the shit, when Summer's baby daddy and his guys jumped him. That nigga Asad can throw them hands too. He was kicking ass for a minute before they got the best of him. Them three soft-ass muthafuckas stomped on his head when he was on the ground. They messed Asad up real bad. They talkin' like he might die from it."

"I read that the police got somebody in the county

for that already. Who got caught?" Promiss asked while responding to a text from Fame asking her if she was free for the two of them to get together later that day.

"Yeah, they said they got two muthafuckas, but Gary went to jail from the club last night for something else. He didn't have nothing to do with it, and I don't know who the other person is. Unless they caught up with one of them niggas after they got away," Shay speculated, then said, "I seen yo' boo out last night too, Promiss."

"See, that's where I know you lying, Shay, cuz I know for a fact that he wasn't all up in All-Stars with you last night. Fame wasn't even in Milwaukee."

"I didn't say I seen him in All-Stars, so stop assuming shit all the damn time and listen. I seen him when we was leaving George Webbs downtown. I was walking out and he was walking in with that Drake-looking dude he be with all the time."

"Slim."

"Yeah, if that's his name. Promiss, you should give him my number. That boy is fine as hell! If the dick good I might have to cuff that."

"Hoe, yo fat ass can't tell me the damn definition of monogamy. In here talking about cuffin' somebody," Endure retorted teasingly.

"Oooh, sooo now, bitch, since you got ole Sharky in your life, you forgot how it is? Or is it that you think you're all that now?" Shay responded. "I'm just trying to find that special special like y'all got. It's hard."

"No, it ain't, Shay. You had a good dude and you kicked him to the curbs for nothing. Screaming that he was trying to control you and shit."

"He was, I don't want a nigga to be all up under me. I want a muthafucka like y'all got, that be out on their grind for days at a time. Just pop in, take a bitch out to a show and to eat, then dick me down good and go get right back at it. That's that thug shit I need in my world. But you bitches ain't tryna hook me up with none of their guys. Why is that?"

"You know what, Shay, I'ma text Fame right now and tell him that you trying to fuck with Slim. So now, bitch, you can't say I ain't did nothing for you," Promiss said, tapping away on her phone.

"Endure, ain't you gonna text Sharky and tell him to put me in with his guy too?"

"See, hoe, that's what I was just talking about. I ain't even been a full sixty seconds and you trying to fuck with another nigga. You ain't tryna be in a relationship for real."

"Yes I am, but you know I gotta have some good dick in my life too. I can deal with an ugly dude as long as he can put it on me right, but I can't mess with a fine-ass dude that can't, just because he looks good. That's unless his head game is right, then we might be onto something." She smiled.

They all laughed, and Endure promised her that she would put in a word with Mister for her. She was surprised when Shay confessed that she already had been messing with him for a week. Shay wanted Sharky to hook her with his friend Zay. All three of them had heard the word around the city about how good Zay was in bed, but he was too busy out in the streets to have a woman at home. Shay explained that she believed they were made for each other, and Endure could not disagree. So she set up a date with him for her.

~ ~ ~

The sturdy power-driven door lock clicked loudly, waking Danny Boy up from his two and a half, closer to three hours of sleep. He got up and proceeded over to the cell door to see what was going on. He did not have an appetite, at least not for county jail food. So if this was for breakfast, he was closing the door and going back to sleep.

"Mays, transport is on the way to take you to intake court. He's already on the floor, so put on your orange top and he's ready to go!" said the morning deputy from his spot standing behind the control desk.

"Alright!" DB responded from his cell's doorway. Then he pulled the door slightly closed for some privacy. He took a good morning piss, brushed his teeth, washed his face, and then slipped on the flimsy shower sandals while pulling the orange top on as he walked out of the cell.

"Mays?"

"I'm ready."

"Okay, line up by the exit," the transport deputy ordered him before going around and collecting the rest of the men on his pickup list.

Once the deputy had everyone he was there for, he informed them that they would be given a bag breakfast when they made it down to court staging. Then he led the seven men onto an elevator and through a maze of corridors until they arrived in front of another control desk.

"Mays, you're up first. As for the rest of you, someone will be around shortly with your breakfast," the deputy explained, locking the rest of the men in a holding cell.

When Danny Boy entered the courtroom, the first thing he did was search the crowd of onlookers that was there to find out the outcome of their loved ones. He found Forever and his mother sitting right in front. He flashed them a quick smile then sat down like we was told by the deputy. Danny Boy did not have a good feeling about the hateful-looking middle-aged female magistrate sitting on the bench in front of him. Next to him at the second table was a big-headed elderly assistant district attorney.

"State of Wisconsin against Danny Mays!" the bored-looking bailiff announced from his place standing beside the bench.

After all of the greetings and instructions were made, the ADA sorted through a thin discovery file briefly before addressing the room.

"Your Honor, I can see no point in dragging this

out in here this morning. The information"—he held up a sheet of paper so the room could see—"reads that Mr. Mays and a small group of thugs beat a man within inches of his life at a night club last night. I have a photo in evidence that so places him there as the driver of the getaway car. I ask that Mr. Mays bail be set at a hundred thousand dollars cash," said the ADA.

When he was done talking about how much of a threat Danny Boy was to the city, the magistrate asked Danny Boy if he needed the court to appoint him a lawyer, then instantly changed her mind and told him that the court would be appointing him counsel. Without giving him a chance to explain his side of the story, the chubby, rosy-cheeked women rushed on.

"Mr. Mays, I am ordering that you remain in

custody of the Milwaukee County Jail on or until a ten-thousand-dollar bail is paid. Next case, please!" she exclaimed, concluding his time with a bang of her gavel.

While Danny Boy was being led back out the way he had entered, he started putting two and two together in his head. He was telling the truth about being at home last night, and he had Forever to prove it. But he would need more than just her word because of the photos the ADA claimed to have of him. He did not know for sure if the state did have photos or not. What he did know is that if they did, then the photos were not as clear as stated because Danny Boy wasn't there. But Freebandz was, and they were both about the same height and very close to the same build and complexion. It would be a real battle for Danny Boy in court. He already knew

Freebandz was not about to step up and take his case. And it was not in Danny Boy's bloodline to rat him out, so this left him in a dilemma.

"Aye, do you think I can get put in a holding cell with a working phone please, so I can get my bail paid?" he asked the deputy.

"You can use the phone when you get back upstairs. I'm taking you up there now," he coolly answered as they passed the holding cells in court staging.

CHAPTER 15

Approximately two months had passed since the Minnesota job, the job that sent a nice flow of good-paying vengeful people in need of Fame's and Slim's services their way. Because or all of the work, Fame and Promiss had not really spent much time together.

This was an issue for both of them. So they set a time and date to spend time together that was mandatory for them to keep every week. This week it was her turn to pick what they did, so she took the easy route and picked a dinner date at the Olive Garden.

Promiss picked the place because they served a

very good mixture of well-cooked dishes that were very pocket-friendly. She did not want him thinking he had to always go big to impress her, plus the Olive Garden was a nice place she did not need to make reservations for.

They were seated at a table for two in front of the window. The glass was lightly tinted, and added with the low intimate lighting, it gave them a feeling of privacy.

"Hellooo, mister?" Promiss sang, snapping him out of his thoughts.

"Come back to me."

"My bad, ma. I was thinking about something."

"Yeah, I can see that much. You're all distracted over there. So tell me what's on your mind." Promiss could see he was hesitant. "Come on, you can tell me," she pressed, giving him a trusting little smile.

The reason Fame was so distracted with her tonight was because his mind was still on the news he received about the shooting and robbery of the eastside gambling house the other night. He would have been there had Promiss not shown up on his doorstep dressed for bed—or more like bedtime sports. The murder of Big Dogg was heavy on his mind, because the two of them were pretty close. They got that way after Fame's father stopped bringing his half-brother, Asad, around.

Big Dogg was not at the spot to gamble: he was the doorman and bouncer. People always sought him out for jobs like that because of his six-foot-six 290-pound frame of stone-hard muscle. And he know how to use it.

"Promiss you already know the answer to that question. Unless you've been lying to me all this time?" he countered, loving to see her smile. Baby, I'm sorry! I was just thinking about my old buddy who was killed in that shooting the other night. You know I would've been there if it wasn't for you coming over."

"So I'm like your good luck charm, or, no, I'm your lucky lady."

She smiled brighter. "Wait, I thought you didn't gamble, sooo why would you've been down there?"

"I don't. Well, not like that anyway."

"Then why?"

"The old head is a friend of the family and he runs it. Every now and then I just go to hang out and to let him know that I'm good out here in these streets."

"And to fuck on them lil bitches down there on the east. Tell the truth," she pressed, still smiling.

"The truth is, it's hard for me to decide on what I

want to eat."

"Are you . . . Really! . . . Okay, if that's really true, then I'ma order for the both of us," she told him, picking up the menu. "Just so you know, by changing the subject, you just gave me my answer."

"No, your crazy ass's just making shit up," he retorted.

"I ain't crazy!" Promiss growled playfully, then smiled and kicked him in the shin under the table.

A waitress appeared and took the order for two plates of scungilli and steak to start with from Promiss. Fame really did not care what it was as long as the meal had meat involved.

"Excuse me, I need to go get something right quick. I'll be right back," Fame said, excusing himself from the table and going out to his car while they waited for their food. "Here." He placed a Kay's gift bag on the table in front of Promiss.

"What's this?" she asked out of pure surprise.

"It's for you," he told her, noticing that all of the women were eying the small gift bag.

"What's it for?"

"You. Because every kiss begins with Kay," he sang jokingly.

"Can I open it now?"

"I want you to. I mean, that's why I gave it to you."

"No, first tell me what you did wrong."

"Nothing." He laughed. "Promiss, I ain't done nothing wrong. I just saw your face when I saw it, and I knew it was meant for you," he answered, reaching across the table and holding her soft hand. Promiss released his grip then anxiously removed the oblong gold gift box from the bag and opened it. She almost forgot to breathe as she lifted a glimmering beautiful pink and white diamond rose gold tennis bracelet. The sight of it got ooohs and ahhhs from the other women. Promiss showed it off proudly to them since they were trying so hard to sneak a peek. At that moment their waitress returned and asked Promiss if it was her birthday. Fame let her admire the bracelet for a few moments before he took it and put on her wrist. There were also matching earrings in the box that she swopped with the ones she had on. Once she had them on she got out of her seat and kissed him like they were the only two in the place. Promiss was still sitting on his lap when the food arrived. She promptly returned to her seat, and they ate, flirted, sipped on a nice white wine, and flirted some more over a pie-like ice-cream dessert.

"Am I spending the night again, or do you have

other plans for us tonight?"

"Noooo, no, no! This is your date to plan, remember?" he reminded her. "And I'm spending the night at your crib. We always go to mine or a room somewhere. So I wanna see how your bed feels on my naked ass tonight. Unless you got something to hide? Some freaky shit that you don't want a nigga to see?" he teased. "I even got my own toothbrush ready in the car."

CHAPTER 16

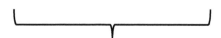

Once again Danny Boy was awakened from his
sleep. This time it was by a short Mexican guy in the
cell next door to his.

"Say, homie, they callin' you for a visit I think,"
he told him while tapping on the cell door.

"Good looking out, fam."

Danny Boy got up and rushed to get himself
together, the whole while wondering who was there
to see him. He had called his mother earlier to asked
her to come pay his bail with the cash she was
holding for him. She told him that he had to wait until
Monday when she could go to the bank because she

could not get that type of money out of the ATM. He had money stashed in his house, but it was not easily accessible for her, and he did not have anyone else he trusted that much to send over there to get it.

Danny Boy got to speak with Forever at that time as well because she was still with his mom from when he saw them in court that morning. Forever told him she had to work that night and that she had told Freebandz he needed to go pay the bail since it was all his fault he was in jail in the first place. He knew it was not Forever there to see him at 7:20 p.m.

"Mays, are you ready to go? You have a legal visit, so head out to the control desk in the hall and they'll tell you where to go from there," the sexy Amber Heard look-alike that was working the unit instructed him when he approached the desk.

"Alright." Danny Boy knew better than to turn

the court-appointed lawyer's visit down. He might need it if things did not go as planned with his bail money, plus he wanted to see what type of quack they'd sent his way. Danny Boy did a quick scan of the men seated in the day room as he made his way out of the exit. "Mays for a lawyer visit," he informed the beefy LL. Cool J-looking deputy at the hall control desk.

"Yeah, Mays, you're down here with me!" the attorney called out to him, then disappeared back into the conference room at the far end of the long hall.

"What up? Why the late visit?" Danny Boy questioned right when he entered the room and sat down.

"Hey, I got the fuck here as soon as I could. Now if you don't want me here, then say so, so I can get an easy check from the city to go fuck off with," the lawyer boldly stated.

"Naw, you cool, man. I was just askin'," the thug responded, liking the man sitting across from him already.

The lawyer introduced himself as Scott Anderson. Danny Boy guessed he was in his mid- to late forties and did not do much public defender work these days. Or maybe he just had a really good side hustle, from the pricey suite and thick gold watch he was wearing.

"Well, Dan. Is it okay if I call you Dan, or what do you prefer to be called?"

"Dan's cool."

"Okay, you're going to have to bring me up to speed on what happened with you because I have not really had time to go over the file. This trial that I'm in the midst of ran late and I wanted to check in with you while I was down here."

"Man, I didn't do shit they're trying to charge me with. I was fuckin at the crib with my girl when they picked me up. I just buried my lil brother the other day, so I wasn't in the mood to be out and about. I did not do that shit."

"I'm sorry to hear about your brother!" Scott told him, then looked over some papers he was holding when Danny Boy walked in. "If that's true, how is it that they have photo evidence that puts you and your car at the scene? And please know that if you're not honest with me, I can't help you."

"I understand that."

"Dan, I don't know if you know it or not, but that guy that got the crap beat out of him is in a coma. If he dies this will turn into a homicide case. So now make me believe what you just told me."

"Scott, I know how shit lookin', but I really was not there. I let a friend of mine use my car. I'm not saying that he was a part of it, because I wasn't there, and I don't know. What I do know is if he was a part of what went down, he's not gonna come in and say that. And I'm not cut like that to tell on him. The only reason why I'm telling you this much is because you're my lawyer and you can't say shit about him if I don't want you too, Right?"

"Okay . . . If what you're saying is true, then the club should have your friend on its surveillance video somewhere. Can you give me a few days to look into things? I believe I can work with what you've just told me and get this case thrown out without saying one word about your friend."

"Yeah, I can do that, but I should be out Monday when they can pay my bail. I'ma let him know what's up just so you know. Scott, I don't know how to be no other way than real. Feel me?"

"I would not ask you to be anything less. Here's my card. Call me as soon as you get out, so we can go over the best way to deal with this."

Danny Boy shook the lawyer's hand after accepting his business card. Then they parted ways, with Danny Boy returning to his cell and the lawyer leaving the building to get started on whatever scheme he had in mind.

~ ~ ~

Forever sat in front of the mirror in Silks Gentlemen's Club's dressing room lost in thought. She was trying to think of a way to get Danny Boy out of jail without breaking herself in the process.

The only place that she could think of to go where she could make $5,000 real quick was a brothel. The only ones in the city that she knew of belonged to a pimp name Mercy Bondz whose son Beysik had been trying to get with her for months.

Forever slammed the rest of her Smirnoff vodka, picked up her phone, and sent a text to Beysik Bondz asking for his help. Then she made her way out to the stage to do her set. By the time she wrapped her thick thighs around the pole, Forever knew she really was ready to have a man she could call her own.

~ ~ ~

Fame was left alone for a few minutes when they made it inside Promiss's house. Right through the door she ran off to use the bathroom. So he went wandering through the place. Fame was pleased with her style and taste in decorating; he was also impressed by how spotless everything was. It was not because he thought she was a dirty person; he just did not think she had the time in her busy life to be so tidy. Fame knew Promiss had expensive taste and had a little money from the first day they met. It's why he approached her.

"Do you want something to drink?" Promiss asked when she returned and found him admiring her family photos that hung on the wall. "Yeah, whatever you got is okay with me," he faced her and said.

"This is a nice crib you got. I don't see why you like coming over to my spot all the time," he complimented her as he walked over to join her.

"Thanks! I like coming to your house because I'm nosey as hell and it's been a long time since I've been with somebody who had his own everything," she said, leading him into the kitchen. "I honestly thought you and Slim were roommates since y'all are together all the damn time." Promiss chuckled then handed him an unfamiliar brand of beer from her large subzero stainless steel and black refrigerator.

"I got love for the homie but not that much. Hell, I'd shoot myself if I had to work and live with his crazy ass," he joked. "I wonder how's it going with him and your cousin. Have you heard anything from her because he ain't texted me shit?"

"Nope, but why are we standing here thinking about what they might be doing when we're supposed to be seeing how you like my bed?" she flirted, taking hold of his hand and leading him into her bedroom where they both wanted to be.

"I see you're ready for daddy tonight." He kissed her soft lips.

"Did you miss me that much today, or is this because I gave you diamonds?"

"Both. Now stop talking about it and make me

cum."

"How about we take a quick shower together and make it our pregame show? I need some hot water on my body to help relax my muscles. I'm kinda sore from my workout earlier," he explained, taking off his shirt and knowing she would not turn him down.

"How about . . . No, better yet, let's take a bath. I gotta big tub," Promiss suggested, watching him wrestle out of his undershirt then revealing the big chest and sexy six-pack abs that she could not get enough of looking at.

"Even better. Lead the way."

"Finish getting undressed first," she retorted lustfully as she sat down on the bed. "I was enjoying the show."

CHAPTER 17

Up good and awake way before the morning sun

could really shine its light, Promiss was lying in bed

ready for another round of sex play with her man.

They had spent all of Sunday pretty much having

themselves a little freakfest all around her house, and

it was those memories that had her craving for more

now.

Promiss laid her head on his chest and listened to

the beat of his heart. The scent of Fame alone was

turning her on more. She squeezed her thighs

together trying to ease the quivering of her swollen

wetness. When his hand dropped to his side between

them, Promiss pressed her mound against it, wanting to feel his fingers massaging her clit the way they had just hours ago. But he was sound asleep, and she really did not want to wake him up, especially after the way he teased her about her high sex drive. But her arousal was not going anywhere with her being so close to Fame's hard warm body.

Promiss got the idea to get Fame nice and aroused as she was while he was still asleep so that when he woke up, he would think it was all him or just be too excited to care who started it. She slowly licked his nipple and eased her hand down under the sheets until she was touching his soft warm shaft. She felt it start to swell in response to her caresses, but he was still asleep. She kissed her way down his abs until she was face to face with the semi-hard thickness that she craved to have buried so deep inside of her at the moment. As Promiss closed her lips around him, she started masturbating, working her clit while sucking on it until Fame was fully erect.

Promiss was so wet that she no longer cared if she woke him or not. She stopped touching herself and sucking on him and just straddled his waist. Then she took his hardness and guided herself down on it with ease. As soon as she was about mid-point, Fame captured her by the waist and started bouncing her up and down while thrusting his hips to meet her. Their impact was hard and deep. Promiss screamed her approval, happy that he was giving it to her just the way she needed him to. She came instantly.

But Fame was not done with her and far from being. He rolled over on top of her and went right back to giving her what she woke him up out of his sleep for.

"I'm cumin! Fuck! I'm cumin!" Promiss sang.

"Give it all to me, bitch. Let me feel it!" he retorted, tossing both of her legs over his shoulders and pounding her harder.

She moaned and screamed louder and louder until what felt like a dam broke open inside her. Promiss had the most explosive orgasm he had given her in the whole day and a half they had been together. Fame's release was not far behind hers; she locked her legs round his waist so he could not pull out and felt his release fill her box.

"Ooooh, bae, why you just fuck me like that?" she questioned in her after-sex glow.

"I had to teach you a lesson about waking up the beast." He smiled. "Did I give you what you wanted?"

"What if I said not everything?"

"What! Really?"

Promiss laughed and kissed him long and passionately before getting out of bed and heading to the bathroom. She asked him to come join her in the shower a few minutes later. Fame turned her down shaking his head and smiling as he sat on the edge of the bed checking his text messages on his phone.

When Promiss returned to the bedroom close to thirty minutes later wrapped in a large rainbow floral-print towel, Fame was not there. She knew he had not left the house because his shirt and shoes were still there, so she started pulling out her outfit for work. Suddenly the doorbell rang twice.

"Bae, could you get the door? I'm getting dressed!" she shouted to Fame, then finished raking down her hair.

"You hungry?" he yelled back as he made his way to the front door. "Who is it?" Fame asked, pulling the door open at the same time. Right away Fame noticed the shocked expression on the face of the man standing there.

"Is Promiss here?" he asked unsurely.

"Yeah, she should be out in a minute. What's your name?" Fame asked, thinking the person at the door was her van driver from work. Promiss had called her van driver to pick her up from home because her car was still at the shop. She did this because her and Fame both said they had meetings to get to in the morning, so this would ensure neither of them were late.

"Drew."

"Bae, who's at the do—" Promiss lost her words when she found herself staring in the face of a ghost from her past. One that was standing there with her new man.

"Good morning!" Drew greeted her cockily.

"Andrew, what are you doing here?" she retorted with anger. "You just can't pop up at my house when you fucking feel like it."

"Wow! This how you talk to me?" Drew asked, looking from her to Fame.

"I don't mean to be snappy, but . . . when did you get in town and why didn't you call first?"

"I did call, and texted you. You didn't respond," he told her, staring down Fame.

Promiss picked up her phone from off of the table beside the door where she left it and her keys when they got in the night before. As soon as she touched it, she remembered that she had powered it down so she would not be bothered.

"Promiss, is this cool here, cuz I gotta get going," said Fame, getting the feeling that the two of them needed some time to sort out whatever this tension in the air was about.

"Yeah, I'm sorry. Could you give me a second to talk to him please?"

Fame did not answer. He just walked away showing his emotion in the way he moved. A few minutes later he returned with his shoes on but still pulling on his shirt.

"P, I gotta go. Call me later." He kissed her on the cheek never once taking his eyes off of Drew. Then he just walked out of the house to his car.

"Sooo I guess he's my replacement, I see," Drew said, watching Fame get into the plum-colored Porsche Panamera and drive off.

"Andrew, let's not do that. Who he is is none of

your business. When I ain't heard from you in over

two fuckin' years. An then you just show up

unannounced at my house like we all fucking good!"

"Promiss you're the one who didn't get my text

because you turned off your phone. So this ain't on

me. I thought you were alone going through one of

your lil spells you be having and shit."

"What the fuck ever! That didn't answer the rest

of my damn question. Drew, look, I don't wanna do

this with you."

"Promiss, this not what I came all the way to

Wisconsin to do with you either." He stepped closer

to her and touched her face.

"Drew, don't," she said weakly. "Whatever you

came for, forget it. As you seen I've moved on, so

what else needs to be said?" Just as she asked, her

ride pulled up.

"Will you just hear me out before you just shut me all the way out?" he pleaded.

"Okay, I guess, but I gotta go now. I'm late. Call me later. Drew I really gotta get going now," she repeated when he did not make a move to leave. Promiss grabbed her keys to lock up and get away from him. He followed her to the van.

"Let me take you where you need to go," he offered once they were beside the van.

"No, I don't think that's a good . . . I can't be late this morning, Drew."

Declining to spend time with Drew was hard to do looking in the eyes of the man who once held her heart.

"Well can I get the consolation prize, then?"

"What's that?"

"Just a hug."

Promiss gave in to him a bit and gave him a hug.

Then quickly pulled away from his warm, hard body.

Having his arms around her just then just did not feel

right to her. Promiss climbed inside the van and

watched Drew get into an Audi A6 sitting on 22-inch

super chrome rims and speed off in front of the van.

CHAPTER 18

When the doors opened for the dayroom's use Monday morning, Danny Boy rushed to the phone tree and called his mother. After his third or fourth try he knew she was not going to answer for him so early in the morning. He dropped the receiver back in its cradle and headed back to his cell. On the way back he decided to go see why all of the guys were crowded in front of the TVs the jail had hanging from the bottom of the upper tier of the cellblock.

"What's going on?" he asked his Mexican neighbor who was also standing out there.

"Oh, they talking about the prison reform bill."

"Anything good being said that's finna help us instead of hurt us?" Danny Boy asked, not familiar with the bill.

"Yeah, it looks like them old white folks in Congress is gettin' sick of paying the high-ass tab to run them prisons. We've been telling them that Truth in Sentencing law was no good for years."

"Yeah, that shit's crazy and unfair as hell. They're giving muthafuckas everywhere from thirty to one hundred years with no parole then crying about it's overcrowded, with their dumb asses."

"Well if they bring back parole or the bill passes, we can earn good time for working and doing programs. Kinda like it was back in the '90s when the crowding problem was solved, and all of them fools up North assaulting the guards and each other will drop."

"Yeah, because them fools will be trying to get that good time and get out," Danny agreed. "Let me know how it turns out. I'm going back to sleep," he said, then turned to head on to his cell. At that time the deputy called his name and told him to pack up for release.

"Aye, y'all, it's happening already!" somebody joked.

Danny Boy laughed along with them already knowing that his bail had been paid and went to collect his court papers.

~ ~ ~

Around noon Drew pulled up out front of Promiss job and parked. He took a nice gulp from a half-pint of Remy and then sent her a text asking her if she was busy.

Promiss was heated, pacing and telling her sister

about her morning's event, with Drew showing up to

her house while Fame was there. As she passed the

window, she spotted Drew's shiny black Audi

parked outside. At the same time her phone chimed

with his text.

"Drew, why you texting me and you're right

outside?" she asked, calling him back instead of

texting. "Don't try and lie cuz I'm looking right at

you."

"I didn't want a repeat of this morning, and I

didn't know if you were still busy or not. Are you?"

"No, but if I was you still texted me, so did it

really matter to you if I was?" she retorted. "I already

know the answer to that because I'm talking to you,"

she said with attitude.

"My bad, P, dammmmn!" Drew apologized. "So

what are you doing?"

"I was just telling my sister about your rude ass."

"Who's that you're talking about me to?" Endure asked with a load of towels fresh out of the dryer.

"This is Mr. Show Up Outta the Blue," she answered, standing in front of the window staring at Drew sitting in the car.

"P, tell her I said wadup." Drew glanced at his watch. "Can we go and get something to eat together right now while you ain't busy, or what?"

"Sure." Promiss thought about using the time to get him to stop coming around. "Yeah, we can. Thanks to you I didn't get breakfast this morning. So, yeah, you owe me."

Promiss gathered her things and thought about asking him to run her to her house to get some paperwork that Endure needed. Then she decided it would not be a good look for her to be back at her place with her ex-boyfriend in the middle of her workday if Fame just so happened to be riding by.

"What do you have a taste for?" Drew asked her over the phone as he watched her luscious hips sway as she approached his car.

"I don't know. What do you gotta taste for?" she responded, ending the call and getting in the car.

"I'm lookin' at what I got a taste for right now." He flirted with a lick of his full lips.

"Drew, don't make me change my mind about this. You know I'm with somebody. I'm only here for the food and to hear you out. Once we put closure to things, then you can move on with your life the way I have."

"Oh . . . Let's get something from Jake's and find a good place to park so we can sit down and talk then."

Promiss agreed then started texting Fame. He had not responded to her or answered since they parted ways this morning. She wondered if he was mad at her about Drew. The ride to the deli was silent because she was too busy texting back and forth with Shay and Endure about the choices she was making.

"So are you going to tell me where you been all this time without me hearing one word from you? And you can't say that you didn't have my number?" she inquired while they waited for the food.

"I was in prison back home," Drew confessed. "I got knocked on some humbug shit that I didn't have shit to do with," he explained at the same time, trying to figure out what Promiss saw in the guy she was with at her house that morning.

When the two of them were together before he went to prison, Drew remembered how she used to tell him she liked his thuggish ways. From what he witnessed, Fame did not fit the type. But he had learned years ago not to judge a Milwaukee boy by first glance.

"You niggas kill me with that same ole shit. It's never you; it's always somebody else or some humbug bullshit." She rolled her eyes.

"Promiss, baby, I'm being serious. I was with you for Juneteenth, remember?"

"Hell yeah I remember."

"Well I didn't leave you until that following Sunday."

"Yeah, so how did you get locked up there if you were here, is what you want me to think, right? But I'm not thinking that way. I mean, Drew, couldn't you have just told the police to call me to confirm your alibi?"

"I got locked up because that old white lady picked me out of a photo lineup and then again in a real one twice. So they wasn't trying to hear shit I had to say. They had both me and the punk who really did the petty robbery that I got locked up for. You know I ain't no rat-type nigga, so I didn't say shit to them bitches. I just drove down on ole boy and told him to take his weight and get me outta that shit."

"Wow, Drew, that's crazy. So did he own up to it, or what did he do?" she asked, observing how good he looked with the few extra pounds of muscle being in lockdown had put on him. She also noticed he was covered in tattoos from the neck down, which made him even sexier to her.

"Naw, he didn't. What's crazy is that old hag that picked me out used to be my middle school teacher.

So that's where she remembered me from. He son, who was also her lawyer, went back to the judge on my trial date and explained to the court that his mother had made a mistake in picking me. He told them that she was having issues with her memory due to her early Alzheimer's. And when he told them she was able to describe me so well because she taught me in middle school, the case got dismissed. Bae, I would've died if I had to do twenty years for some shit I wouldn't stoop low enough to do. I ain't never with robbing little old ladies at gas stations and shit."

Right then their order was called. They drove to Miller Parkway Park and continued to talk about everything that had been going on with him while he was gone. It was so easy for Promiss to fall back into the familiar place with the man beside her. She fingered the bracelet Fame had given her just a few nights ago.

"What do I do? What do I do?" she screamed in her head questioning her torn heart.

TO BE CONTINUED

All praise be to God, Lord of my world! Now to all of you that're close to me, you know my life has been a living hell. It's because of all y'all and the loyalty between us that clearly has been forged from the many hard life lessons we've endured together— the happiness, hardship, and heartbreak that we've experienced together—that I have the fuel to write this fire. I'm still trying to get better and better: to perfect my pen game and learn how to get out of my own way. So I thank you readers for your love and support. I can't forge your honesty. I thank G2G for giving me the chance to see my long nights of writing become the book I dream it to be.

This book is dedicated to:

Club Fed 089-090
Lorenzo Summerville RIP
Wendell "Doc" Baker
Jim "Ray" Jones III

To order books, please fill out the order form below:
To order films please go to www.good2gofilms.com

Name:_____

Address:_____

City:_____State:_____Zip Code: _____

Phone:_____

Email:_____

Method of Payment: Check   VISA MASTERCARD

Credit Card#:_ _____

Name as it appears on card: _____

Signature: _____

Item Name	Price	Qty	Amount
48 Hours to Die – Silk White	$14.99		
A Hustler's Dream - Ernest Morris	$14.99		
A Hustler's Dream 2 - Ernest Morris	$14.99		
A Thug's Devotion – J. L. Rose and J. M. McMillon	$14.99		
All Eyes on Tommy Gunz – Warren Holloway	$14.99		
Black Reign – Ernest Morris	$14.99		
Bloody Mayhem Down South – Trayvon Jackson	$14.99		
Bloody Mayhem Down South 2 – Trayvon Jackson	$14.99		
Business Is Business – Silk White	$14.99		
Business Is Business 2 – Silk White	$14.99		
Business Is Business 3 – Silk White	$14.99		
Cash In Cash Out – Assa Raymond Baker	$14.99		
Cash In Cash Out 2 - Assa Raymond Baker	$14.99		
Childhood Sweethearts – Jacob Spears	$14.99		
Childhood Sweethearts 2 – Jacob Spears	$14.99		
Childhood Sweethearts 3 - Jacob Spears	$14.99		
Childhood Sweethearts 4 - Jacob Spears	$14.99		
Connected To The Plug – Dwan Marquis Williams	$14.99		
Connected To The Plug 2 – Dwan Marquis Williams	$14.99		
Connected To The Plug 3 – Dwan Williams	$14.99		
Cost of Betrayal – W.C. Holloway	$14.99		
Cost of Betrayal 2 – W.C. Holloway	$14.99		
Deadly Reunion – Ernest Morris	$14.99		
Dream's Life – Assa Raymond Baker	$14.99		
Flipping Numbers – Ernest Morris	$14.99		

Flipping Numbers 2 – Ernest Morris	$14.99		
He Loves Me, He Loves You Not - Mychea	$14.99		
He Loves Me, He Loves You Not 2 - Mychea	$14.99		
He Loves Me, He Loves You Not 3 - Mychea	$14.99		
He Loves Me, He Loves You Not 4 – Mychea	$14.99		
He Loves Me, He Loves You Not 5 – Mychea	$14.99		
Killing Signs – Ernest Morris	$14.99		
Kings of the Block – Dwan Willams	$14.99		
Kings of the Block 2 – Dwan Willams	$14.99		
Lord of My Land – Jay Morrison	$14.99		
Lost and Turned Out – Ernest Morris	$14.99		
Love & Dedication – W.C. Holloway	$14.99		
Love Hates Violence – De'Wayne Maris	$14.99		
Love Hates Violence 2 – De'Wayne Maris	$14.99		
Love Hates Violence 3 – De'Wayne Maris	$14.99		
Love Hates Violence 4 – De'Wayne Maris	$14.99		
Married To Da Streets – Silk White	$14.99		
M.E.R.C. - Make Every Rep Count Health and Fitness	$14.99		
Mercenary In Love – J.L. Rose & J.L. Turner	$14.99		
Money Make Me Cum – Ernest Morris	$14.99		
My Besties – Asia Hill	$14.99		
My Besties 2 – Asia Hill	$14.99		
My Besties 3 – Asia Hill	$14.99		
My Besties 4 – Asia Hill	$14.99		
My Boyfriend's Wife - Mychea	$14.99		
My Boyfriend's Wife 2 – Mychea	$14.99		
My Brothers Envy – J. L. Rose	$14.99		
My Brothers Envy 2 – J. L. Rose	$14.99		
Naughty Housewives – Ernest Morris	$14.99		
Naughty Housewives 2 – Ernest Morris	$14.99		
Naughty Housewives 3 – Ernest Morris	$14.99		
Naughty Housewives 4 – Ernest Morris	$14.99		
Never Be The Same – Silk White	$14.99		
Shades of Revenge – Assa Raymond Baker	$14.99		

Slumped – Jason Brent	$14.99		
Someone's Gonna Get It – Mychea	$14.99		
Stranded – Silk White	$14.99		
Supreme & Justice – Ernest Morris	$14.99		
Supreme & Justice 2 – Ernest Morris	$14.99		
Supreme & Justice 3 – Ernest Morris	$14.99		
Tears of a Hustler - Silk White	$14.99		
Tears of a Hustler 2 - Silk White	$14.99		
Tears of a Hustler 3 - Silk White	$14.99		
Tears of a Hustler 4- Silk White	$14.99		
Tears of a Hustler 5 – Silk White	$14.99		
Tears of a Hustler 6 – Silk White	$14.99		
The Last Love Letter – Warren Holloway	$14.99		
The Last Love Letter 2 – Warren Holloway	$14.99		
The Panty Ripper - Reality Way	$14.99		
The Panty Ripper 3 – Reality Way	$14.99		
The Solution – Jay Morrison	$14.99		
The Teflon Queen – Silk White	$14.99		
The Teflon Queen 2 – Silk White	$14.99		
The Teflon Queen 3 – Silk White	$14.99		
The Teflon Queen 4 – Silk White	$14.99		
The Teflon Queen 5 – Silk White	$14.99		
The Teflon Queen 6 - Silk White	$14.99		
The Vacation – Silk White	$14.99		
Tied To A Boss - J.L. Rose	$14.99		
Tied To A Boss 2 - J.L. Rose	$14.99		
Tied To A Boss 3 - J.L. Rose	$14.99		
Tied To A Boss 4 - J.L. Rose	$14.99		
Tied To A Boss 5 - J.L. Rose	$14.99		
Time Is Money - Silk White	$14.99		
Tomorrow's Not Promised – Robert Torres	$14.99		
Tomorrow's Not Promised 2 – Robert Torres	$14.99		
Two Mask One Heart – Jacob Spears and Trayvon Jackson	$14.99		
Two Mask One Heart 2 – Jacob Spears and Trayvon Jackson	$14.99		

Two Mask One Heart 3 – Jacob Spears and Trayvon Jackson	$14.99		
Wrong Place Wrong Time – Silk White	$14.99		
Young Goonz – Reality Way	$14.99		
Subtotal:			
Tax:			
Shipping (Free) U.S. Media Mail:			
Total:			

Make Checks Payable To: Good2Go Publishing, 7311 W Glass Lane, Laveen, AZ 85339

CPSIA information can be obtained
at www.ICGtesting.com
Printed in the USA
LVHW041546050320
649105LV00010B/914

9 781947 340442